MW00422604

HELLO, HORSE

Richard Kelly Kemick

Hello, Horse

Stories

A JOHN METCALF BOOK

Biblioasis
WINDSOR, ONTARIO

FIRST EDITION
10 9 8 7 6 5 4 3 2 1

Library and Archives Canada Cataloguing in Publication

Title: Hello, horse / Richard Kelly Kemick.
Names: Kemick, Richard Kelly, 1989- author.
Identifiers: Canadiana (print) 20230573886 | Canadiana (ebook) 20230573894
    ISBN 9781771966078 (softcover) | ISBN 9781771966085 (EPUB)
Classification: LCC PS8621.E595 H67 2024 | DDC C813/.6—dc23

Edited by John Metcalf
Copyedited by Sohini Ghose
Cover and text designed by Ingrid Paulson

Published with the generous assistance of the Canada Council for the Arts, which
last year invested $153 million to bring the arts to Canadians throughout the
country, and the financial support of the Government of Canada. Biblioasis also
acknowledges the support of the Ontario Arts Council (OAC), an agency of the
Government of Ontario, which last year funded 1,709 individual artists and 1,078
organizations in 204 communities across Ontario, for a total of $52.1 million, and
the contribution of the Government of Ontario through the Ontario Book
Publishing Tax Credit and Ontario Creates.

PRINTED AND BOUND IN CANADA

And what horse shall I ride?
The dark one. The bright one. The one
without eyes.
—Michael Prior "Richmond"

THE STORIES

PERFECTION

The 5th Race

I forgot to tell you this, but it's incredibly important. Her grandfather was Joseph Malta, one of the two hangmen for the Nuremberg executions. She would take me to his house for dinner when we were working doubles, and we'd watch him bumble around the kitchen, serving cucumber sandwiches with Earl Grey. I never asked about his past, but it seemed to dangle in the air, straining with its own weight.

After the hangings, he moved to Tallahassee where he returned to work as a floor sander and lived in a bungalow with no hot water. He didn't care about my parents or my career prospects or my intentions with his granddaughter, who—even from across the table—could be heard grinding her teeth. He cared only about the dogs. Again and again, I'd tell him that I didn't know, had never actually seen a race since that was the best time to muck the kennels. But his granddaughter, I said, was allowed into the track's inner circle and watched the hounds wheel the corner for their final sprint home.

He ignored her and leaned towards me. "This world," he said, "is not fit for man nor beast."

At seventeen, I could hardly be called a man—could hardly be called much of anything. But since his granddaughter was in her early twenties, perhaps he assumed I was too. Or perhaps he had seen such horrors by the time he turned seventeen that he assumed there wasn't much growing up left for me.

We left him with the dishes and biked to the Presbyterian parking lot to blow tendrils of pale smoke into each other's hair. Across the lot, three girls sang "Double Dutch."

"I want to see fireworks," she said, then paused for a coughing fit. "I need to see something explode."

I held my breath. On the exhale, I replied, "We could put a pear in the microwave."

Behind her, the girls sped their tempo until the rope snapped and blurred.

By the time we returned to the track, the veterinarian was waiting. "You know," he told her, tapping his watch, "vet techs are a dime a dozen. Six months and they churn you out like butter."

"Bit of a mixed metaphor," I said, to which he told me to go fulfill myself sexually.

I watched her follow him to the kennels. She had all the trappings of beauty but was actually quite ugly. Yes, she was thin, had distinguished features, with skin so soft and pale you'd paint your bathroom that shade. But she was also anaemic, had a brutal bone structure, and skin so white it was as if light no longer touched her, like one of those creatures who lives at the bottom of the ocean and whose heart beats once every hour.

I checked in with my boss, who was dipping each of his rings into a paper cup filled with vinegar. At that time, he'd either just got parole or was just about to break it—I forget which. But I don't forget the small seam of kindness running through him, a seam that the world was bent on exploiting.

"Did you talk about the trials?" he asked, rubbing each ring with a rag until the silver burned. He asked me this after every dinner, and after every dinner, I'd respond with the negative.

He torqued the rings onto his fingers—including his thumb—and then pointed at his computer. On his screen were greyscale photos of dead men on wooden planks, blood like potpourri over their faces. "It says here the trapdoors were too small. Each man dropped face-first into the wooden sides." With his shined hand, he lightly slapped his cheekbone.

I said, "Do you have a pear I could borrow?"

I was cleaning the bathrooms, buffing the hand dryers so slick there wasn't any need for me to polish the mirrors, when my walkie-talkie beckoned me to the operating room. The OR was where the vet inspected each dog before a race, checking heart rate, joint movement, and for any signs of doping. The check was state law, but the vet never took it seriously. More often than not, he wouldn't even show but just get his tech to forge his signature on the form and fit each dog for a muzzle.

The operating room was empty, save her. She was washing her hands in the sink. "I didn't find a pear," I said, "but I got—"

She turned and showed her smock was covered with vomit. She smiled.

Earlier that summer, she adopted some Eastern religion, one with uncountable gods with uncountable arms. "The scriptures say," she had informed me, "that the moment this world achieves perfection, we will no longer need heaven. And heaven will cease to exist."

"No offence," I said, "but I don't really believe in angels. Aside, of course, from organized crime."

She was bemused as she shook her head. "It doesn't matter what you believe in. If heaven disappears," she said, and her smile backtracked into a frown, "we will have no one to believe in us."

In the operating room, she shimmied out of her smock, dripping vomit onto the tile.

"What'd you give him?" I asked.

"Three tablespoons of laxative." She dragged a bare finger through the brown-green puddle on the stainless-steel table. "This isn't even the start of it."

A white greyhound named God Speed had begun racing a couple years prior, and since he was only sixty pounds, he was expected to caboose every race. But instead, he won. Nine races a year, one every other week in summer, for two full seasons. This was his last year, and he'd won four races already. There were only five remaining.

I opened a package of rags. "Don't you think you've gone a bit far?"

She shook her head. "The perfect season, the perfect career. The perfect dog. It cannot happen."

"Does my tongue taste like a coral reef to you?"

"Without believers, even the Divine does die."

God Speed was racing in the evening's nine o'clock slot. A track is 565 yards long, and a hound can lap that in thirty seconds.

As we scrubbed the OR spotless, the overhead speakers popped on and the announcer began his colour commentary. I couldn't understand any of it, except the rising crescendo of his voice until he was screaming into the microphone and the crowd turned feverish.

"God Speed!" he yelled. "God Speed!"

The operating room smelled like bleach, like the very end of time. She buried her face in her latex gloves as I peeled my boss's hard-boiled egg.

"All I want," she whispered, "is to save the world."

That night, our heartbeats turned into ticker tape as we biked Tallahassee's northern hills. We slept spooned-up on the grass, and when we awoke the dew glistened on us like gold.

The 6th Race

That was the week I urged her to phone in sick, but she said destiny was depending on her.

In the OR, she struck a stately pose as I painted her face blue. We were supposed to use some sacred mixture of ash and hyacinth, but having only a cigarette's amount of the former and all but none of the latter, I used a blue whiteboard marker we'd lifted from the front office.

"This seems a bit much," I told her.

"The gods require much," she replied.

"No, I mean I doubt real people actually do this."

The blueness of her brow highlighted her eyes, which swelled with terror. "Do not say we are not real."

She closed her eyes and began to pray. I had faked a workplace injury to get the prescription that would transcend her to the celestial plane where, she assured me, her other blue-faced gods played croquet with the planets.

"Stop grinding your jaw," I said. "I don't want to get any on your lips." I looked at the marker. "This might be toxic."

As I hosed the kennels, I heard the click of nails on concrete. I turned around but didn't see anything. I had unplugged the overhead speakers to give us some quiet, and the only noise was the distant crowd and water trickling into the drain. I drank deeply from the hose.

I heard the nails once more and spun around—again, then again, then again. On a dry patch of concrete, the flowers of paw prints.

"Do you see these too?" I asked, but the kennels responded by saying nothing. Through the slit of the window, a wind picked up, and I closed my eyes to let the breeze whisk the water off my face.

"Why are you crying?"

The vet was standing in front of me.

"It's the hose," I said, kinking its flow.

"Do you know where she is?"

I shook my head.

"Well, when was the last time you saw her?" His voice was so slow, I felt the seconds thicken.

"I don't remember."

"Well, tell her," he said, "that God Speed had peanut butter smeared all over his gums—" he pulled back his lip with one hand and pointed to his gum line with the other "—and he could not stop licking."

I ran my tongue over my own teeth and found them all solid.

"It's a miracle," he continued, "that he still won. Tell her—"

"Do you see these?" I asked, pointing at the paw prints.

He looked down. "See what?"

I pointed harder.

"What? Your footprints?"

My eyes widened with otherworldly wonder. "May the saints save us," I said, but he checked his watch, spat on the concrete, and left.

She was curled in the back kennel. "Wake up," I told her. "Wake up. The dogs are coming."

I rolled her head upright, and her tongue slugged out of her mouth. The blue marker was sweating off her face and her cheeks were checkered from the chain-link.

"They're almost here. Wake up."

How many times do our worlds end?

"Wake up, wake up."

And she did.

The 7th Race

The sore on her jaw had opened again, and the red caught the light like a ruby. Her foot was jittery on my chair as her fingers thrummed her thighs, her whole body squirming out from under itself.

But Joseph Malta didn't notice. He was dangling a tea bag above his Earl Grey. He fidgeted with the paper tag, and the bag slowly rotated, rusty water dripping from its face, as he awaited an answer to a question I'd already forgotten.

"He made the drop too short," my boss told me. "The fall's supposed to snap your neck, but they didn't fall far enough. So they dangled. Strangling." He tapped his screen with his pinkie ring. "One guy, Jerlitz Fruster, took thirty minutes—thirty minutes!—before he finally passed out so they could just shoot him."

I sat on the chair beside him, and together we watched a video of the trial. I rested my head on his shoulder and inhaled his lavender cologne. And as the British judge read the pronouncement of the coming plunges, I confided in him that history was too cruel for my liking.

"We need to be reminded," he said, restarting the video, "reminded of the sixty thousand lost."

I sat upright. "That's it? Seems low."

He clicked around on his computer. "Maybe it was million? Sixty million."

My head back on his shoulder: "That's better."

Constellations of cigarettes were scattered around the parking lot ashtray, and I swept them towards the storm drain. She crept behind me and put her hands over my eyes.

"What the fuck's on your fingers?" I said, struggling to pry open my eyelids.

"Vaseline," she said. "I'm testing it."

As I rubbed away the thick light, I saw her shadow leave for the operating room. "Wait," I called after her. "Are my eyes open the same amount?"

After God Speed raced blind to his seventh win of the season, she decided not to get sad but get sunny.

Behind the kennels, not a human soul around, the floodlight tapping with insects: on the other side of the corrugated steel, the dogs smelled us and started to whine.

We stared into each other's eyes, giggling uncontrollably, and took turns slapping each other in the face. Gradually, our limbs dropped to black like banks of lights in a warehouse. When we could no longer lift our arms, we started swinging from the socket.

The whines turned into barks which turned into yelps. She smacked me with a dead-fish fist, and my right eye swelled shut. In response, I corkscrewed my body as far as my spine allowed, and let my arm soar through the air and land hard across her mouth. A tetherball of red arced in the lamplight, and the kennels screamed as the dogs threw themselves against the wire.

Her face uprighted. Her eyes wet with joy. Her teeth and lips clown-faced with blood.

The 8th Race

I had been mopping the concession all afternoon before my boss pointed out there wasn't any water in my bucket. I was shocked by how smooth the yellow plastic was. "It's like the skin on her heel," I told him as I stroked the bottom of the basin. He nodded, slowly.

I collected my "Caution: Wet Floor" signs and wheeled the bucket towards the tap in the bathroom. In the women's washroom, she jabbed her fingers into my ribs.

"Don't do that!" I said, spinning around. "You'll pop my lungs."

From her breast pocket, she produced two white pills.

"They're not pills," she corrected. "They're Q-tip tops." She took the cotton swabs and, holding my chin, slid them into my nostrils.

"Is this supposed to be fun?" I asked.

"No," she replied, "it's supposed to be hard to breathe." She smiled. "Hard to race."

"But I can still use, like, my mouth."

In the bathroom's hard light, her face crumpled. The speakers crackled on for the nine o'clock showing.

I still don't understand the thrill of the race, perhaps because I've still never watched one. But I know that the dogs keep chasing the lure well beyond the finish, and there's a perfect pain in that.

The announcer's voice was a sphere of sound. He told us that we were special and beautiful and it was a wonderful time to be alive. And he told us God Speed had shattered the track record by a full quarter second.

The 9th Race

We pedalled past the city's cage of light pollution. My mind was full of fireflies, but hers was someplace else.

Earlier that evening, my boss described the elementary school gym. "I mean, they did it right there. Where kids had played badminton, eaten snacks. Afterwards, they burned it to the ground." He noticed the clock and left to get an early seat for God Speed's career-closing race. "I'll empty the garbages for you on my way," he said, leaving me alone in his office. And as I emptied his wallet, I believed I would never see him again. I also believed the garbages would be the last nice thing he'd ever do for somebody. But when I ran into him decades later in a bar in Tulsa, I was incorrect on both counts. He introduced me to his wife, a bottle-blonde who had pen-palled him letters, and when I asked them for money, he gave me one of his rings. And to his wife's scowling objection, he said, "My fingy's too fat for it anyways."

When I entered the OR, a scalpel was on the table, the blade shining in a blossom of blood.

She didn't make me ask. "I cut his paws. Right across the pad." Her red hands held my cheeks. In the corners of my mouth, I tasted the dog's heart. "Why are you crying?"

Halfway through the northern hills, she skidded her bike onto the shoulder by a roadside payphone. The small screen blinked

8:59, and we held hands until the digits switched to 9:00. In under thirty seconds, destiny would arrive.

Beneath us, in twinkling Tallahassee, I could almost see the race unfold. The slips swinging open, the lure throttling along the rail, the cameras flashing, and then the sightline of the final turn, lips brandished white, tongues hung through wire muzzles, eyes so desperate with desire it is all they know. And while they do not realize it, the finish line approaches.

9:01.

That was also the day Joseph Malta had spilled boiling water on himself. I had thrust his hands into the sink and opened both taps to cold water, and as I stroked an ice cube along the hands that once held the rope that once held the world, I looked over my shoulder.

At the kitchen table, eyes shut, letting the evening light cut between the venetians and fall straight through her.

"This world is not fit for man nor beast."

9:02.

Nothing had changed, except her shakes were now from relief. "I'll call the track," she said, "to see what he placed. Maybe third, or even last."

I turned to Tallahassee. The uncountable streetlights glowed like all of heaven's haloes.

She picked up the phone. But there was no dial tone.

My hand back in hers. Beneath us, street by street, the lights of our city flickered to black.

HELLO,
HORSE

B y Christmas break, the snow had been falling all
month, and the drifts now bury the statues of
people nobody knows. Jeremy and I turn onto
the slice of Trans-Canada that cuts through town, and we find
the blizzard has emptied the street.

Since 'tis the season, public works have hung light-up crosses
beneath the streetlights—but to save on electricity, they've
switched off the streetlights themselves. And the crosses are
glowing hospital-white as the snow spirals through the empty
street. Jeremy's skinned knuckles slip by mine, so close I'm not
sure if we touched. In the moonlight, my bare legs look like
birch trunks beneath my black dress, and the daisies stitched
around the neckline are tight against my collarbone. I'd usually
wear a sweater and jeans, but my dad wasn't called in tonight,
and I knew I'd need his permission to go. But I also knew that
his heart would shatter like a falling icicle at the sight of his

daughter—of her own free will—splendid in the only piece of clothing he's ever bought me. "Millicent," he said, "have fun."

We round a corner, and two blocks in front of us, the wind tangles itself around a figure in the middle of the road. He is standing perfectly still, his eyes squinted shut. His right hind leg bent at the knee and limp at the fetlock. He is asleep.

It's really not that rare. Because of all the cattle around, the breeze blows their high-octane hormone feed out into the dirt, and the fatty clumps draw in wild horses. Ranchers hate them because one'll break into a paddock and sex everything that moves. But what the ranchers swear is even worse is that afterwards, the herd has to be broken all over again, like they found out something they were never supposed to know.

And here is one now, on the corner of Main and Schmirler, the crosses shining the snowflakes fluorescent. Sleet has caked across his ribcage, where his fur is the thickest, and the long bow of his neck curls his head downwards.

But if you've never seen a wild horse before, you've got this all wrong. They're shrunken, almost dwarfed. They've got this patchwork coat that's stitched across their bodies. Matted manes, chipped hooves. They're as majestic as a stray dog. But they have that beauty that comes from never being close.

The wind shifts and he startles. His hoof slams against the asphalt, and Jeremy's hand jumps onto mine. The horse pivots to stare at us, shuffles his hooves, and snorts two smoke-stacks from his nostrils.

I try to pull Jeremy but he's rigid.

The horse explodes into motion. His hooves thrum against the road like a drumroll. I tug Jeremy's hand but he clenches tighter.

The snow slides from his body in sheets until he is a dark, dark brown. His breath breaks on each stride, keeping the drumroll in time.

He's not moving. His hand frozen on mine.

I can see the flex of his muscles. The white ring around his iris. But at the last moment, he peels to my left and stampedes past, so close that if I wanted, I could reach out and graze my hand along his flank. Hello, horse.

I swivel with him and my face feels the ribbon of heat trailing behind. He gallops down the street, past the spotlight of crosses, and disappears. I hold my breath to listen to his hooves fade, the drumroll slowly dying.

Jeremy drops my hand and I ask if he's okay, but he only comments on how cold it's got. The wind wrings the water from his eyes and freezes it in long lashes. A supple shade of purple frostbites his lips, his bloodied knuckles shine like ruby rings. My snow queen.

• • •

When Jeremy and I were thirteen, his dad got his arm sheared off by the front blade of a rock-saw. Right from the shoulder. But the saw had spent the last fifteen minutes buried in silt-stone, so the metal was so hot that it cauterized the wound as it made it. An arm's lopped onto the dirt and a shoulder socket's a dead-end, but there isn't a drop of blood. Everything had been burned closed and probably smelled like hamburger.

The crew called an ambulance and by the time it showed up Jeremy's dad was sitting upright on the bumper of the half-ton, cradling his bad arm with his good. Once they got him to the site hospital, the doctor said reattachment was impossible since the joint had been soldered shut, but he couldn't believe a wound that bad didn't mean blood loss. So, just to be safe, he ordered a blood transfusion, and someone on the crew was a match.

Jeremy's dad started acting all loopy, but the doctor said it was because he was still in shock. Then, out of nowhere, he sank into a coma. The next day, Jeremy was called down to the principal's office where his mom told him his dad is dead.

Turns out the doctor didn't read the form right and was pumping O positive into him even though he was O negative, which—as Jeremy's dead dad demonstrates—isn't so hot for you. It comes out later that the doctor had prior negligence claims, but the oil company kept him on because of the shortage.

The company gave Jeremy's mom $63,750 for the arm. Then they gave her $337,500 for the rest of him. It's odd to think your arm is worth, like, 20 percent of your body. Seems a bit much, no? But Jeremy says there's this piece of paper somewhere that has it all written down, so when everyone's losing their minds over lost limbs, lawyers just go to the spreadsheet, drag their finger down the column, and find the figure.

It's been three years since his mom got the payout, but Jeremy says she's blown it all. Though she still dresses rich. She wears this red fox coat—even when it's warm out—and some femme-fatale lipstick that smears over her teeth. She smells like car freshener. Jeremy tells me dinner is usually a cold can of something but his mom'll open it while wearing pearls. The white spheres against her clavicle as she struggles with the can opener.

• • •

The snow crunches beneath our feet at every step, as if it's apologizing for something. Jeremy is walking so goddamn slow I can tell he's embarrassed.

"Have you found out anything new for our great Vancouver escape?" I ask.

He tries to keep his excitement reined in, but I can tell it's there. "Just a couple things," he says and starts going on about their Pride parade, like I haven't heard this a million times before.

"The whole city shuts down, Mill. The whole fucking city."

I've been thinking lately about a place called Rivière-du-Loup. I thought about pitching the idea to Jeremy though I know he wouldn't bite. But I'm not upset—I hardly know anything about the town, just its name. River of the Wolf.

"It's so different on the coast," he says. "If you beat up a gay guy—even if you don't know he's one—you get charged with a hate crime and put away double. They love fags like me."

Whenever we're alone, Jeremy's always saying stuff like this. But I've seen how he really is—how tonight at the party he stretched his neck from side to side when Natalie was losing herself over Patrick's blood on the linoleum, and how afterwards Jeremy put his hand on her shoulder (his ruby rings right by her face) and said he was sorry for startling her and then tucked a lock of her hair behind her ear with inhuman gentleness. I want to believe him—I do, because it's the secret that gives our friendship weight, keeps us from floating away. But I'm not sure the secret is real, if the truth isn't really a lie.

Last year, I was at the pharmacy buying cough syrup with codeine to take over to Patrick's. We were dating at the time, and he was on RiteSave's no-sell list. Up in the ceiling's corner was one of those curved mirrors with a fish-eye reflection. I could see into the neighbouring aisle, the one filled with lube and Baskin Robbins–flavoured condoms, where a man stood, his shoulders pulled inwards, holding a small box that looked delicate against his hulking frame. My dad.

Until that point, a part of me believed that when I wasn't with him, my father vanished, waiting in the ether until I returned. Seeing him here, separate from our home, made him appear like an animal outside its habitat, alone and in over its head.

I stared at him as he stared at the condoms, his wedding ring glinting in the drugstore light. He then looked over his shoulder, pretending he was stretching his back, and slipped the box into his pocket.

At first, I didn't believe what I saw. But as he walked past Tammy at the cash, the automatic doors parted before him, unknowingly complicit, I began to understand there was another dimension to him, one that throbbed with hunger. In the aisle between the contraceptives and the first-aid supplies, I began to understand my dad existed unto himself—not to love me or to hate me, but simply because he was alive.

Jeremy and I turn down his side street, the light of the crosses shrinking behind us and the wind is sharp against my legs. Christmas lights line all the houses except his. The vinyl siding sags from his bungalow like loose skin.

I follow him through his gate and watch him unlock the back door, listening for the click. He lets me into the mudroom and my rimed legs burn. I tap my boots on the mat that reads: "Love is a four-legged word." Downstairs, there's a rustling and a light turns on. Jeremy tells me to wait as he goes to talk with his mom.

Two picture frames hang from the coatrack: "Horse People are Stable People" and "D-O-G is G-O-D looking in the mirror."

I hear their conversation but can't make out what they're saying. Her voice is higher than I remember, shrill even.

On the wall hang several sets of fake antlers, each with a wooden parrot perched atop. A felt cat wraps his paws around the doorknob. Beside him, nailed to the door, is a poster of a guinea pig emerging from hay, with the caption: "Who you calling Pig?"

Jeremy and his mom don't own any animals.

Finally, the basement light switches off and Jeremy comes upstairs.

"I'm sorry," he says. "She got up to take a sleeping pill and wouldn't stop asking questions."

"About what?"

"She wanted to know what the girls at the party were wearing."

"What did you tell her?"

"Tube tops and fur hats."

"Did she ask what I was wearing?"

He grabs two beers from the fridge, and we creep down the hallway towards his room. Jeremy moved into the master bedroom after his dad died, and his mom took over Jeremy's old room in the basement. On the front of his bedroom door, hangs a small sign that says: "The deer never studies the body of the tiger." I point to it. "What the fuck does this even mean?"

He shrugs. "My mom got it for me. I think it's a bad translation."

"You know," I say, "most people would have a sign that says *Jeremy's Room* or *No Girls Allowed*."

He follows me in and closes the door. His walls are postered with his owl drawings: a spotted owl in flight, a burrowing owl with its head poking out of the sand, a snowy owl in a cedar. My favourite is still the barn owl on the fence post, wings unfurling, sketched in the half second before flight, its blank white face impossibly clean. Above his dresser, there's a watercolour of a great horned owl I haven't seen before.

We sit on the foot of his bed, and I sip my beer but can feel my stomach mounting rebellion. I lean back onto the bed, hoping that he will turn on top of me, but he doesn't. Just stays sitting.

I excuse myself to the ensuite bathroom. Women are always freshening up. Maybe I'm not fresh.

Growling at the mirror, I see a green glob between my canine and whatever tooth comes before the canine. I use Jeremy's dry toothbrush to dislodge the gunk and carefully inspect the evidence. When was the last time I had broccoli? I think back to the meat pie my dad force-fed me as I was leaving, as if all that stood between me and certain death was "just two more bites."

I exit the bathroom, and Jeremy is sitting in a chair by the shut bedroom door. The chair is so close to the door that we should've bumped it on our way in. He tilts his head back and drains his beer, then tosses the empty bottle between his cut-up hands. I cross the room and sit on the foot of the bed.

I ask if he wants to make out, but he just stares at the bottle, and I'm too nervous to ask again. After a moment, he turns the bottle upside down, like a miniature club. Watching the drops fall onto his jeans, he mumbles, "Take off your clothes."

I snort a laugh. When he doesn't say anything, I ask, "Can't we kiss a bit first?"

Still fixed on the bottle's brown glass and his raw knuckles wrapped around it, he whispers, "Millicent, just take off your fucking clothes."

I don't want him to think I'm frigid. I also don't want him to think I'm scared. I stand up and dance a little, peeling off my socks. I toss them onto his lap but he's a statue.

I stop moving. "I need help with my dress. The zipper in the back. I can't reach."

He doesn't move.

I struggle it over my head and let it crumple to the carpet.

Jeremy stands and looks at me for the first time since I came out of the washroom. He takes off his T-shirt and undoes his jeans, stepping out of them when they collapse to his ankles. Both of us are now in our underwear, standing four feet apart, staring at each other, like some shitty lingerie ad.

He bends over, grabs his jeans and T-shirt and tosses them to me. He snatches my dress from the carpet and throws it onto his bed.

The room holds a calm and pacing violence, something you'd feel inside a zoo. I think back to the party—the blindsiding slur and then Jeremy hitting Patrick's face well after the boy lost consciousness, well after Patrick's top teeth punctured through his bottom lip. And my mouth, too, has been stitched closed.

Jeremy goes to the bedroom door and shoves the chair aside. He then flings open the door, and I cringe at the bang. He walks back to the bed, passing so close to me that the fabric of his boxers brushes my thigh, and—if I wanted—I could reach out and clench a fistful of their cotton and pull him towards me. But he's at the bed, lying fetal on my dress, his bare back facing me.

The open doorframe stares at me like an eye with its eyelids pulled open. I'm shivering so I still my body by hugging Jeremy's clothes.

"Jeremy? P-Patrick doesn't know you're…I mean, I'd never tell."

He just curls tighter, and through his window, I see the snow ascend off the rooftops like holy light.

I let myself out, closing the bedroom door so there's no click. I dress in the hallway. The T-shirt fits baggy but his jeans are surprisingly tight. Before I leave, I press my ear against his door and hear the squeal of a zipper.

• • •

Last summer, just days after Jeremy's sweet sixteen, some guy on his death bed, in a lung-cancer confession, wheezes that the rock-saw wasn't an accident. He says he found out that Jeremy's dad was a closet-case and that he swung the blade just to scare him but didn't mean to slice him, and then—to assuage his guilt—he donated his own blood.

Overnight, Jeremy's mom went from the stoic widow to the woman who stops the whispers when she enters the curling club.

I never see the dress again. A week later, my dad wants to take me out for Christmas dinner. Real father-daughter shit. I put on black pants and a white blouse. I look like my mom and he says so too. He asks about the dress he gave me for my birthday, and I tell him it got stolen out of my gym locker. He phones the principal and yells at her answering machine for like half an hour.

I've still got Jeremy's shirt and jeans in the back of my closet. They're even washed and folded, in case he wants them back on short notice. In class, he acts like nothing ever happened. And, come to think of it, nothing did.

• • •

Ms Haxton once told us that the wild horses here aren't really wild at all, just generations of livestock turned feral. She said the only real wild ones are endangered somewhere in Mongolia, but she told us this five years ago, so they're probably all gone by now. There's no real wildness left, just a handful of animals that ran away.

"The deer never studies the body of the tiger." Does it mean that it's easier to believe you can get away from something when you don't know what it's capable of? So I've stopped looking at this town and have succumbed to the merciful white of snow blindness. But the restlessness of deep night is another story. After waking up from your dad's bedroom lamp flicking on and watching his footsteps in the light that scalpels beneath your door, what else can you do but open the cabinet of your chest and bring out your crystallized moments to polish them for a spell?

Jeremy is straddling Patrick, his knuckles pulling ribbons of blood from the boy's mouth, until I extend my hand onto his shoulder and he freezes. Like I'm his snow queen. Fist cocked, he looks at me with eyes red and blooming like roses, and I can see how tiring it must be to hold on to what's wild and let go of what's not.

WHAT DESCENDS
WHEN THE LAKE THAWS

Twenty-five, and I know more about the world than all my ancestors put together. Where the oceans stop. Where the deserts wait. Brother told me that in the map's blank spaces, they used to draw monsters, but now there's only men. If they came back—my relations, I mean—I don't know how I'd explain such a thing: that on a sheet of paper, no bigger than a desk, is everywhere you could ever be. But if I could choose (and I've thought about this a lot), I'd switch with them. Seems to me that everyone before us knew themselves. There was nowhere else to go, just be still. They must've been as clear as the water you walk on.

1872, Dominion of Canada. In the footprints of Mackenzie's mad dash to the sea, came a lesser known—though no less mad—dash to the mouth. To name. To ink up the atlas with labels and legends and great grids of ownership.

The whip hands of empire had seen the value in creating a world that we could not speak of without speaking of them. And if you could prove that you knew a place—had seen it and scaled it—they'd let you have it if you called yourself theirs.

Picture the territory as a winter boot. 49th parallel as the sole atop America, the coast of Henry Hudson's bay as the laced-up tongue, and the eastern tip of Rupert's Land curls into toe cap. Near the ankle—where the skin stretches—two lakes: Great Bear and Great Slave. Both so deep that when you're born your mother skips a stone, and the day that stone stops its pendulum to the bottom is the day all the clocks of your world stand still.

Yellowknife has two streets. They do not meet.

A sampling of stores:

- Provisions
- Hotel and Tavern
- Provisions
- Boat Repair (closed until spring)
- North-West Police
- Provisions
- Provisions
- Gun and Ammunition
- Provisions
- Dene Hunting Guides
- Provisions

Nothing to buy but ways to leave, and in the tavern we are overstaying our welcome.

I say, "Brother, the Queen cannot stand anything the Americans share. Not even the church."

"Not even God?"

"Great Bear is wider but a trapper told me Slave is deeper. The greatest lake in the territory. The greatest lake that's all ours."

"If it's so great, why they call it Slave?"

"For reasons we well know, Brother. Bastarding. The name ain't right. From the Slavey people—"

"How much for another round?"

"More than we've got. But do you know what they gave that pigeon-livered Thompson? Or Fraser? Or Hearne?" (I don't mention Franklin.) "All we need is two thousand feet deep and we prove the lake is greater than anything in America."

"So we wait for summer."

"Out there? On the big water? The wind'll flip you like a flapjack."

"I ain't the one who can't swim."

"Think, Brother. The ice makes it easy. We go out, find two thousand feet, and they'll grant us a title. Call the lake whatever we want."

I let that sink in.

"Twin Lake."

"Cordin Lake."

"Fraternity Lake."

"Cordin Lake."

"Slavey Lake."

"You're drunk."

What is the nature of all ambition? Like water, I suppose. Bottles up fine by the fireplace but step outside and she will crack you open chest to chin.

Few years back, I was waiting out the rain in a Seattle gallery and the top hats were too scared to *shoo* me. I studied each painting until I became it: angels wrestling on a rock, a schooner splitting the waves, a horse standing in a room of gold.

But what was I to do with all these lives worth living, and mine set apart?

We buy a dogsled without the dog.

"Why no dog?"

"Woof."

Hay River is two hundred miles distant on the southwest shore. Twenty days, we cut a path along the ice to take a cross-section of water, come clean out the far side.

Grandmother always said, you are the things your surround yourself with. If such be true, here is what we are on the sled:

- Fishing line, with hook and lure
- Half barrel of jerky and dried berries
- Leathered deer lung of kerosene
- Sulphur matches
- Tin bowl
- Hatchet
- Ledger and pencil
- Tent canvas and poles
- Snowshoes
- Eight sheets of wolf fur
- Musk ox coats with badger hoods
- Snow-blind goggles of walrus bone
- Caribou mitts
- Compass
- Ice-fishing drill (a telescopic pole twisting a four-foot corkscrew)

But above all: we are rope. A half-mile's worth. We are every stretch of it for sale. Horse hair, burlap, cotton fibre, even an arm's length of silk—such a fine braid. Swiped it off an Indian agent while Brother haggled over mukluks.

On the sled, the rope coil stands tall as our hips. Brother climbs into the centre, squats invisible.

"Join me!"

I hunker beside him. We turn giddy in our well, walled with rattlesnake.

We sell what we are no longer:
· Four fingernails of gold from Dawson
· Sluicing pans
· Pickaxe
· Two-piece bridle
· Ruby ring we unfingered from a corpse in Fort Simpson
· Breastplate from the Whitehorse mines
· And of course, promises to return, wealthy and generous

"God takes 10 percent," said Grandmother, a Salt Laker, smoothing a wrinkled bill onto the table. Deep in nameless territory, Shoshone been pushed into Pacific, the closest souls around were the ones above.

Outside in the sun-scorch of Utah summer, Brother was belly-down in the dirt, watching the lettuce underleaf, rot darkening the heads. The inland sea rested unseen but you could still taste the sting of it.

Frost came quickly, and we came hungry. I caught Brother in the garden, having wormed his fingers for phantom potatoes and found only dirt, so he ate a mouthful. Had he no shame?

No chagrin? No desire to die without dirt between the teeth? I put my boot on his head and ground his face to ground.

In the morning: Grandmother at the table, still as bone.

In the afternoon: we dig her beneath the garden.

Brother threw a fistful of dirt onto the bedsheet. I took one myself but, curious, touched it to my tongue. Salt.

And I knew I was wrong for having put my foot to his face. For he was only tasting what he knew we would never return to.

Standing at the mouth of Yellowknife River, we step our snow-shoes onto the lake's snow, which squeezes two feet thick till ice. I have harnessed myself to the sled, trailing at a distance, all our supplies in the coil of rope.

I have heard it whispered that in the coldest months, the lake does sometimes move. Plates of ice quake, and the newfound water smacks the air just long enough to take the world in but shuts itself before anything can struggle to surface.

If the lake takes the sled, I can't be close to it.

Out before me, a long throw ahead, Brother carries the ice-fishing drill, so valuable it must be held. The steel frame is cinched like a cross against his back. And out before him, a white tightness seals the planet.

It makes you quiver how quick the shoreline leaves you. By mid-morning, even a telescope couldn't spot you a tree. There is only the sound of our whimpering steps and the wind's scribbles.

We slant south by southwest, walk till noon. Brother tells the time from how the sun breaks the sky like a whale surfacing to breathe. The drill holds our handful of sunlight with blinding holiness, and I wear my walrus-bone goggles. Peering through slits, the world becomes thin, simple.

We trudge until the moon hangs.

Brother extends the drill and twists the screw into the ice. After three feet, he falls forward on account of the sudden softness. The water gushes up to greet us, happy and gossipy.

In one half of the hole, I try and take a trout. In the other, Brother feeds in the rope.

But the rope floats.

His voice tight, he says, "How did we not consider this?"

We have nothing to weigh it down. Compass, tent poles, drill, hatchet—all of it too precious to risk.

"What about a stone?"

He throws his arms to show our new world of nothing. "Where do we get a stone?"

I search my own person—gloves, boots, my wiggly molars. Nothing to stay sunk.

We are a one-day walk from Yellowknife, but the idea of retreat is heavy enough for everyone but the rope.

"Use the hatchet."

"If it doesn't come up, you're going down for it."

Hand-over-hand, Brother lowers the rope.

I take a trout.

The rope relaxes and there's that blinking terror of not knowing if the hatchet has loosed or if the bottom has risen to meet it. Brother tugs and the rope tightens. We exhale: there is still something for gravity's grasp.

He throws a hitch and hauls the rope to surface. Hatchet dripping prehistoric mud. The rope, already stiff with frost, flattens against the ice, and Brother measures the drill (four feet to the eyelash) end-over-end. We want two thousand feet.

I open the seal skin pouch I carry around my neck and dig out a sulphur match, strike if off my thumb, light the kerosene in the tin bowl. I skewer the fish with a tent pole over the flames.

"How long?"

"One hundred and sixty-two feet."

A tad shallow.

The fire spits.

"We'll go deeper."

In the tent, between our planks of wolf fur, I weep with homesickness. But where is it I am sick for?

Each day, time overlaps, thicker and more the same.

Yes, the planet spins around the sun, but the planet itself also spins, so is it not possible that if you walk at the right pace in the right direction, you can remain in the same spot with all the world moving beneath you?

The stone skyline of Utah, and our skin turned the colour of cloud. Brother and I baited skunks into the shed where we would lengthen our days with the claw side of the hammer.

The snow began and did not stop. We turned twelve and foraged for brumating snakes. Unearthing them, ten or twenty would roll over each other, and I knew they'd do the same in my own stomach.

So when the Mormon man came, collecting tithe and his saddlebag jingling, Brother and I roused ourselves to see the hammer's claw, drip-drying in the shed, sunlight through the slats.

Hand-over-hand. Trout in the fire.

"How long?"

"Three hundred ninety-nine."

A tad shallow, the fire spits.

"We'll go deeper."

Driftwood like hands hidden in snow. I hack free some splinters to dip in the kerosene where we dip in our fingers. Singe the skin until the cold feels kind.

All this in silence, save for the ice which has begun to speak— or rather, sing. Deep and lilting, like a tabernacle choir.

A story we heard while train-hopping on the spur line from Provo, Utah:

By the time we arrived, racoons are dancing their gloved hands, surgical, through the married mother of three. So gentle. If Captain's horse hadn't broke a leg and begged for a bullet, we'd have arrived that morning: seen first the flies; then the crows; then the coyotes pair up with the daughters and tug them to ribbon; and the black bear who nibbled the tongue clean out the boy's mouth. But nothing touched the man, his sun-creased skin. And our pyre's flames worked him long into evening. There is a hardness in this country that exists only in us.

I find pleasure in piercing the ice. A torturer taking confession.

"How much?"

"Three hundred eighty-four feet."

"A tad shallow," the fire spits.

"We'll go deeper."

On our backs, we watch the borealis. The colours toss across the sky: pink and green. Brother is amazed by their soft motions, but I've seen the like before. That time at Lake Tahoe when

Brother shoved me off the dock, and soon I'm at the bottom, looking up to see the way light moves through water.

We each have a moose bladder that carries a couple quarts. But sweating beneath fur cultivates a wild thirst. I try shoving snow into the sack to warm against my belly but turn myself to shivers.

Instead, when we drill open the ice and the water comes babbling, we fall to fours and lap like deer. Slurp until ice reforms and we are kissing crystal.

So quick you forget what flowers smell like, the scream of insect wings, the caress of a dry towel.

In my dreams, we are shunted to the tavern of Hay River, victorious. The blossoming breath of whisky, a fly walking across the wet, a hand laid on shoulder blades.

I startle awake, thighs wet, having forgot that I have forgotten these things, which—I suppose—is its own form of remembering.

"How much?"
   "Four hundred even."
   A tad shallow. The fire dwindles.
   All we need is two thousand feet. All we need is the bottom to give.

The grizzly floats across the snow.
   Standing upright, its eyes and mouth shut dead. From beneath the hood of its face emerges another face. "You two a long way for fishing."
   "How long it take to fix that skin into a coat?"
   "Not long. Their bodies 'bout same as ours."
   "How far till Hay River?"

"Six, eight days."

"You mapping the lake?"

"I'm hunting bear."

"I thought they hibernate."

"They do, 'cept the very strong and the very sick."

"Doesn't appear to be anything out here with us."

"Don't be a fool. Prey is scarce so they cut across the lake."

"How you haul them back?"

"Bit of black powder, blow open the ice, and push their bodies in. Holds them for spring when me and Peggy boat out from Resolution and tow them back."

"You're shittin' us."

"Did it once and a prospector looked at our towline and said, 'You whaling out there?' Peggy said, 'Yessir.' We winched the first carcass from the water, prospector looked and said, 'I thought whale sharks live only in the tropics!'"

Yuk yuk yuk.

"You boys stay safe."

"Doesn't appear to be anything out here with us."

The bear turns and skis eastwards, his rucksack bulbing his back, rifle slung atop it.

"Wait! You got a rock for us? Anything that'll sink."

Shrug. "You'll find nothing sinks this far from shore."

All day long, the lake sings. Brother far ahead, the sled far behind. The ice is cleared of snow, and small bubbles ascend with each trill, pockets of air pinned against the glass like the empty circles of whole notes.

I have seen culture. In San Francisco, Brother and I snuck in an alley door, looking to loot some silverware but stepped backstage of a theatre and found myself snared by a woman, spotlit.

Black feathers from her body. Each tiptoe like she was stepping free from gravity. How to express the way the light held itself on her throat? How to convey that she spun lighter than thought? How to say that I wanted to hold her, not for anything savage or cruel, but solely for the chance to rise alongside?

The violins screeched and she collapsed against the stage. I turned to Brother, ready to find him pillaging some closet, but saw him beside me, his face soft with pain. And I knew then that we would never leave each other, that we were two wings on one body.

At night, I listen to the crinkle of snow on the tent. Each flake, like a finger tapping against a fish tank: "Is anything alive in there?"

Hand-over-hand, trout in my mitts.
    "How much?"
    Too much wind for fire.
    "How much?"
    "Three hundred fifty-six."

A story we heard at the train station in Pocatello, Idaho:

Billy was on the bar, spent, seven petals of red blooming his face. Room gone still as lantern-light in deer eyes. Animals, all of us. The bartender uprighted the chairs, dancers swept up the glass. The boy starts plucking the baby grand but he's a half-beat slow, somewhat sorry—though not at the far, far distance we find ourselves from grace, but since Billy wasn't done telling us of the men of the unmapped territories who know nothing of our lives.

When I piss, I cannot find my pecker. I am burrowing into myself. Open a square inch of skin and coax me through.

I get the runs. The wind freezes the mess to me, and I am greatly embarrassed crawling into the tent with water on my face, but he somehow knows.

"I am the same."

The gales are merciless, and the ice shivers, and my kneecaps are still. The lake hits castrato and I turn around to the opening of a fault line, steam roiling off the water, and the sled becomes buoyant.

Water touches the fur, the sled disappears, and my harness yanks me.

Slide across the ice, feet first, nothing to hold, bite off my gloves, jerk the harness, can't break the frozen knot.

The worst part will be how long the dive will take.

Driftwood catches my heel. The anchor of everything we are sucks the air out of me.

Brother is charging past, screaming, "The rope! The rope!" and I watch it slither into the water.

He kicks off his snowshoes, flings off his furs, and dives naked into the fault.

The driftwood starts to splinter. The harness winching my chest. The driftwood cracks, gives, catches my hip. The harness wheezes out my last gasp. The red silk, an umbilical cord attaching me to the next life.

The harness.

The harness has a buckle. Course it does. I grasp at my back, tug and jerk, and the weight of the world is stripped off me.

Scramble to the edge and push my face below the surface but the water is so cold I can't see.

Time is a knife standing on point.
Our lung of kerosene bobs to the surface.

Atop a boxcar bound north, Brother is sitting with a stray cat in his lap. He is thirteen. The sun drags last light across the prairies. The swaying of the train causes his and the cat's eyes to close.

He gasps at the surface, his hands breaking the panes of water. His eyelashes freeze him blind.

I roll him out and onto his nest of clothes. Pour the kerosene on his chest and dig out a sulphur match. Strike it off my thumb.

Light him on fire.

The screams pump the blood, makes him thrash out the flames. I lay myself over the ember of his body and seal in his warmth.

Darkness is long. We have no idea when we wake.

What the water has eaten:
· Sled
· Quarter-barrel of jerky and dried berries
· Tin bowl
· Tent canvas and poles
· Eight sheets of wolf fur
· Snow-blind goggles of walrus bone
· Compass

What the water never touched:
· Snowshoes
· Musk ox coats with badger hoods

- Sulphur matches
- Ice-fishing drill

What the water has returned:
- Leathered deer lung of kerosene (but now empty)
- Ledger and pencil, waterlogged and illegible but with the fishing line and lure tangled around

And another thing: held beneath the ice, like an artifact behind museum glass, the rope is spiralled at the surface, hatcheted to bedrock.

I tink-tink-tink the ice open with the drill's point, and the sound is like the time we opened up that drunkard's skull to see what thought looked like. A fist-sized hole, just enough to pull the rope free. I thread it through the coil, throw a hitch, and drag the rest, wiggling out the hatchet.

"How much?"

The drill, end-over-end.

"Three hundred fifty-one."

Brother, convulsing with cold, points eastwards to where the bear hunter departed. Set of ski tracks like ruts leading us to a future we cannot escape.

A half-day's trek, and the tracks stop where sheets of ice have collided, overlapping into a range a mile long and twice our height. We bellycrawl to the top and right there—on the leeward side—is the bear hunter, facing away. He's stood his skis upright in the snow to sit with his back against them. Having lunch, perhaps.

I whisper to Brother that maybe, somewhere, the hunter blew open a hole for one of his kills and that sent the shiver through the ice that nearly ate us. But he—still crippled by chills—calls me a liar, says that we shouldn't sin before sinning.

The sun is breathing at the horizon's surface and we wait upon its exit. I slice the deer lung into strips and we chew the leather like cud. The tang of kerosene sets our strength.

I tomahawk the hatchet but the blunt side hits his head, the thud dulled by bearskin. He whirls around, lunging for his rifle, but I'm on top of him, unhooding the cowl and his skull is pink and smooth and I slam it against the ice.

"Wait!"

Brother is behind me. The rope slung around him like a planet's ring. "Why is the lake so shallow?"

I cock the hunter's head to face him.

"It's not. D-d-deeper the farther east."

Above us, crows circle.

"Don't leave me here. Please. D-d-don't let me freeze."

Gently, I roll him to face the lake.

"Wait. What is a—what wussit—whale shark?"

"I don't know." A bruise flowers around his mouth.

Brother nods, and I bring the flower to the ice.

A story we heard on the northern shore of the Boise River, Idaho:

Goshawks have these locking claws. You understand? Bones like gears. The bird can't let go until it's landed and steps out the guts. But when they hold too much? Bad drought one year and Ox Lake disappears. The lake bed reveals a hundred drowned hawks, claws gripping what they have to hold.

Approach one and just when you think there's no life left, the fish tail smacks.

Brother becomes the bear.

What the rucksack has that we need:
· Hard biscuits and caribou jerky (we eat without chewing)
· Sulphur matches

What the rucksack has that we do not need:
· Small keg of black powder
· A bone knife, sharp as sin but no bigger than your thumb
· A novel called *Roughing it in the Bush* (skimmed a few pages but seems dry)
· Feather of an unknown bird

What the rucksack does not have that we need:
· Tent

The skis fit neither of us, so we hatchet them to tinder and the book starts a fire that stands two feet tall. I curl in the windbreak of the rucksack and watch hell dance in Brother's eyes.

He says, "Fourteen days to Lutselk'e. Dene settlement on the eastern arm. We're travelling light."

"But only a four-day retreat to Hay River."

"We have more to measure. And it gets d-d-deeper the farther east."

"But—"

"Was it me who wanted this? Was it me who begged? Was it me who was you?"

What was the life that awaited me in Hay River? The crescent left by a glass on the counter.

We break camp eastwards. The rucksack fits everything, and I sling it over my shoulders. Brother is ahead, carrying his cross. Leave the black powder, leave the gun. The only thing we'd shoot is each other.

First, your legs burn. Then, your lungs. Last, Lord forgive us, your whole body.

We try the bone knife but it floats. So we're back to the hatchet.

Hand-over-hand.

"How much?"

The wind whines.

"How much?"

The rope limp at the surface. The hatchet has loosed.

I am worried, then, that he will kill me.

But he takes off his mitt, roots beneath his coat, and presents a gold locket.

"Where'd you get that?"

"From the rucksack."

I am worried, then, that I will kill him.

But he ties the locket to the rope. Hand-over-hand in. Hand-over-hand out. Measures with the drill.

"How much?"

Loses count. Starts again.

"Six hundred twenty-two."

I untie the locket, and I expose my hands to elements just so I can open it. A tiny picture of a blonde-haired woman. Her eyes will soon see the centre of the earth.

Time is our stomach. We wake when we're hungry, stop when we're starving, rip open a fish.

My first week on the ice, I could never will my mind to stillness.

But now? By the time we get to the fish's tail, scaly and thin, I am already halfway into that other world, that warm and cloudy water, so tuned to the heat of a human body I don't even feel it. And I am at the sandy bottom of Lake Tahoe. And I am seeing how light moves through water. And I am seeing a hand reach down to me.

The sun rises in a clear sky. We lie face down in a snowbank, afraid to look on a world of white fire. Ear to the ice, the lake hums its tune.

I roll onto my side and float out an eye. Blinding and unnatural, and it's because the sun has split into three separate circles. A beaded string of light.

"What's wrong?"

"Am I still alive?"

Brother's pinky snaps off. Went to piss, gloves off, pissed, gloves on, and an odd look on his face. Exposes his hand, fingers frostbitten into talons, and from the stump: no blood, just a bit of crude.

I use both mitts to scoop it up, and we have returned to Grandmother's garden, gathering earthworms. "No need be gentle, boys. See?" She pulls one into two and both halves still wiggle. "Like you in the womb."

We are both thinking the same: What's that taste like?

The drill snugs to the hilt. Ice is too thick, so we shelter behind a snow dune.

Brother opens the bear at the throat, bares his chest, and snarls on the silk rope as I lance his boils, dab them with snow. These are the marks I fired onto him.

"Like the Devil's trying to get out."

His chest burned by flames, his face burned by cold.

That night, I wake to a lynx, wet nose to wet nose. I clutch at it, but only take a fistful of air. So light on the snow it doesn't leave prints.

I open my eyes to a dark room in Missoula. Those final moments before the life you left catches up, hits you like the claw side of a hammer.

From the darkness: "Don't turn on the lamp."

"Brother?"

"Don't turn on the lamp."

I turn on the lamp.

"Good god."

"I said don't turn on the lamp!"

"What have you done?"

I turn off the lamp.

"Tell me what you've done."

"I don't know."

I found him then, in the darkness, and washed his body with warm water. The cloth in gentle circles until his nakedness shone in the moonlight, his heart throwing itself against his breastbone: an animal too big in a cage too small.

A story we heard at the saddle shop in Great Falls, Montana:

The boys say a lady can't break a horse, only teach it tameness.

Ms Kitty haunts my stables of late, begging me a mare to take her south. Mr Walthrop's been sipping gin again, and her jaw's cracked and coloured like stained glass. But I say, "Turn the other cheek," since I'm a lady who well knows her Bible. And that's also how I know all shall be forgiven when that night I break Mr Walthrop in the mud and find some space between his ribs, just thin enough to welcome in my spurs, a small bit of tameness, a little bit of light.

"How much?"

"Nine hundred eighty-two."

Every day closer to two thousand. I can taste the numbers being said.

The fishing line pulls so hard it nearly pulls me in. Brother and I wrap the line around our mitts.

"Onetwothree heave. Onetwothree heave."

Out flops a crayfish, thick as thigh. We set upon our catch, scales frozen to our nails, blood thickening our beards.

The fish twitches long beyond dead.

We lick the red off the snow.

If I remember right, there's supposed to be islands in the eastern reach. Big ones, with trees and birds and winter berries. But there've been none.

Ahead, Brother consults a sky that is no longer there. No sun, no moon, no stars. What's above us is as deep as what's beneath.

Tell me why in some stories the words come easy? You are watching a man to be hanged and the trapdoor swings and the rope snugs and the term "jigging" forms in your mouth. Or the two bull moose fighting, and you describe their eyes as "Old Testament violence" and even though Brother mocks you, he does so only because he, too, understands. Grandmother in the morning, the fly on her eyelid trying so hard to wake her, working its many-legged magic.

But in other stories, the very opposite is true: the most straightforward of scenes—a grizzly, still sick from summer, charging towards Brother's back—is rendered tongue-twistedly obscure, so much that you are strapped into silence, not because of cowardice nor anger nor even some twisted delight, but because you have quite simply forgotten its name.

But the lake does not forget. Brother uprights and turns to face his future—an arm's length away—when the ice forms a mouth and swallows them whole, as if they are the same word.

Brother is straddling the border, a leg on either side.

"Canada, America. North, South. The future, the past." Eyes wide as planets. "Two places at once."

My blood in my heart, my blood in his.

So what, pray tell, do I do?

Do I leave him, stumble towards the shoreline where I'm picked up by a dogsled, towed to Lutselk'e and sleep for three days to wake-up anew, and in the slush-ice spring, catch a ride with Peggy—blonde hair in the wind—to find a bear floating at the surface but know there is another one, far deeper, which the current has stood on his feet?

I do not.

Do I vow to carry on our mission, and plod throughout the night to lower the rope twenty-seven hundred feet (a full furlong more than needed), and return to town where I am heralded as a harbinger of great triumph, and kneel before the Queen, only to rise as governor and proclaim that the lake has become Bear?

I do not.

Do I do nothing at all because after the night of the lynx I never woke up and have been damned to drift across this wasteland, the fires of judgement freezing my eyelids open?

I do not.

Do I throw my naked body across the hole, suspended in the steam, before I dive into the unfeeling water, and the grizzly swims up past me—leaving paw prints of bubbles—and I see a circle of descending darkness, the shadow I cloaked him in, and hand-over-hand do I chase him to the bottom of a lake that will stay forever named after a people who do not exist?

I do.

I think of the globe. Not the planet, but the globe. You see the difference? The planet's everything there is. The globe is everything there is with lines drawn over. And within those lines there are entire civilizations who do not know the feeling of waking up to see that it has snowed.

PATRON
SAINTS

The evening we arrived in Paris, a Bengal tiger escaped from a circus in the city's densest neighbourhood. An announcement was made in the adjacent subway: « Un tigre est en liberté. S'il vous plaît quittez la station, » and there was that two-second chuckle before passengers realized it was real and stampeded up the stairs, their feet mauling a woman who, hobbling on a full-leg cast, could not keep pace.

The shepherd and I descend from the upstairs apartment to open our used bookstore at nine, not a minute later than the frosted glass promises. The return flight touched down in Winnipeg late last night, and I have nothing but affection for our hand-painted rules on the front door: "No Solicitors, No Bare Feet, No Self-Published Poetry." The first two in Milton's writing; the last, in mine.

On the Persian rug by the register, the shepherd figure-eights over my feet. Her joints are so rusted that she no longer lies down but collapses. She exhales and says she can still smell the Seine in my shoelaces.

"They're cleaning it up," I say. "No longer pumping sewage into it."

She says, "Aren't the sewers there famous?"

I say, "There, everyone is famous."

We are interrupted by the door's sleigh bells, jingling the entrance of a young woman who wants to buy a book. The one Milton wrote.

"I gave my last copy to my mother," she explains. "But she said she loved it too much to let it go."

"What did Rilke write?" I ask, gravely, passing her a copy from behind the counter. "In love, we need only to practice letting go. For holding on comes easily."

"Is it true that he works here?"

"No."

She hands me a pillar of toonies. "Oh, I was told he did."

"No," I repeat, counting her change. "He died in 1926."

The woman leaves, and the shepherd says, "You know that—"

"Yes," I say. "I know she wasn't asking about Rilke."

"No," says the shepherd. "You know that I will never judge you."

The Paris bookstore was so crowded that the manager emptied the freestanding stacks so people could peer between the rows. All eyes on Milton as he read from his fancy French translation:

Et son corps commençait à vieillir en avance rapide et mira-
culeux, sa peau durcissait et grisonnait, devenant un bâtiment
médiéval dans lequel les docteurs faisaient promener leurs
instruments stériles en cherchant un battement de coeur.

At the back, I cracked open one of the display's hardcovers
and searched for typos—a feat difficult to do with my toddler-
level French.

After Milton had autographed his way through the coiling
lineup of fans, we were chauffeured to our friend Jen's apartment. Jen was in Nigeria for four months, slurping up the last
puddles of oil, and had mailed us the keys to her Latin Quarter
condo.

I unpacked while Milton, naked on top of the sheets,
checked-in to his 6 am flight.

"Remind me your itinerary," I said.

He sighed. "Paris to Brussels to Zurich for the French translation; Berlin and Munich for German; Madrid and Barcelona
for Spanish; Dublin then London for the original. Ten days
until I'm back here, and then you and I are Paris to Winnipeg,
via Chicago."

I undressed, lay down beside him, and the closeness of our
skin softened his impatience.

"Sure you won't change your mind?" he said. "I mean,
change it again. The publisher will pay for you to come."

"Absence makes the heart grow fonder," I said, curling into
him. Across the Atlantic, I heard the shepherd finish the Dean
Martin song: "...for somebody else."

Hours later, I awoke to the blue halo of his cell phone glowing his face. He has forgotten how to sleep, like it is a second

language he learned in high school. I touched his inner thigh and said, "Tell me what you want," but he wrestled with the child lock on the prescription bottle, and soon enough his breath had turned bitter and deep.

In the morning, a kiss on the forehead, and I listened to his suitcase *clack-a-clack* across the two-hundred-year-old hardwood. Then, the thud of the wheels, counting each stair for the two stories down. I looked out the bedroom window, to where stripes of sunrise spilled across the cityscape, and there was no difference between gold and stone.

I hold the shepherd's hips while she tries to shit by the tree. Beneath my hands, I feel the pain working its way out of her body.

The shepherd says, "In the Middle Ages, a human came home to see his baby gone and his greyhound's teeth bloody. The human stabbed the greyhound only to find the baby safe beneath a mattress alongside the chewed-up body of a viper. Peasants heard of the dog's martyred death, so they made him a saint. Saint Guinefort."

I say, "The most surprising thing about the dog saint is that there's only one."

I wanted to tour the city like Charlemagne, a visiting conqueror in a land unknown. But the avenues were designed after a spider web, and I didn't know the words for help. Instead, I took to each street like it was where I was supposed to be and soon stood gobsmacked before eight metres of stained glass, through which sunbeams radiated onto the street like fingers pointing to select the saved. And within the windows: scenes of angel wings and tiger teeth.

All last night, there had been sightings. A slip of orange behind the carousel, a flash of eyes in the streetlight, the twitch of a tail between headstones.

Commuters roiled around me, but as the crowd churned, I glimpsed a woman on a short stool, her back to me, sketching the scene within a window's corner.

She felt me hovering over her shoulder. « Q'est-ce que vous voulez? »

"Are they playing cricket?"

She glanced back at me. "It is Cain clubbing Abel."

"Have you heard about the tiger?" I asked.

"Everyone has heard about the tiger."

She was a teacher and—after I questioned more—revealed she taught art at a studio in the southern end of the city.

"And why are you in Paris?" she asked.

"I'm waiting for someone."

"And how long will you wait?"

"Ten days," I said, and blushed at how absurd that sounded, how frail. Milton once called me an emotional anvil, but I've always felt more like a leaky bucket in a fire brigade, spilling at the slightest jostle.

She closed her sketchbook on the first murder. "That is a lot of time," she said, "to buy me a lot of wine."

Of course, I thought I had charmed her, had been brazen in a way I couldn't have been back home. In time, I will admit this was not the case. But I believed it then, as I believe it now, as I believed it later that night when she said she couldn't sleep with someone else in the bed, and so I slept on her floor, on a comforter at the foot of the mattress, curled up and without shame.

Walking up the stoop to the bookstore's door, the shepherd's front paw slips, and she keels forward. I scoop her up, and it's like carrying a seventy-pound bag of mud and scrap metal. I take her in my arms and lay her on the Persian rug.

The shepherd says, "Don't be sad. Think of how much less you'll have to sweep."

I say, "You're only thirteen." She is fourteen, but I want to make her feel young.

She says, "And all the money you'll save on lint rollers."

I say, "This is just a phase," and she says, "I never knew you believed in reincarnation."

Then, in hardly more than a whisper, she says, "Tell me something that will change my life."

I tell her that sperm whales have hearing so sensitive that when they dive to the ocean floor they can hear the throbbing of the earth's molten heart.

She says, "How about Cheetos for breakfast?"

I say, "We've got Cheez Whiz in the staff fridge."

And so we sit in tongue-slapping silence, our backs against the front desk, eating radioactive light straight from the jar.

In the early morning, the sky bled purple as we shuffled around her sixth-floor apartment. The kettle screamed on the hot plate, and she stubbed her toe on the table's single chair. The bathtub and oven in the same room.

"Do you think the tiger survived the night?" I asked.

"I need money to buy breakfast," she said. "You made me sleep late."

I found my jeans and peeled some bills out of my wallet. "Who creates art this early?"

"People with jobs."

Before she left, she pushed aside a stack of hand-painted postcards and drew me a map of the city: a circle with the Seine frowning through.

"We met here," she said, pointing at the frown's buck-tooth island. She then circled other locations: the Eiffel Tower, the Arc de Triomphe, the Louvre.

"Do they have the painting of dogs playing poker?"

Searching for the tomb of Napoleon, I wound up inside a basilica and watched tourists take selfies in front of saints guarded by velvet ropes. Hoards rubbed St Peter's bronzed foot, and when their hands parted I saw that the toes had been massaged by so many that they'd been worn into leprotic nubs. Near the altar, a man waited—all casual—for the security guard to pass and then laid his hands upon the face of a sandstone Gabriel. His fingers slid down the archangel's pocked chest, and I recalled how it felt to be beneath Milton's palms and stay perfectly still as he moved over me like rain across a hot sidewalk.

Pricing some Munros, I come across a copy of *Who Do You Think You Are?* and am reminded of when Milton demanded the same of me. We were washing dishes, and as time wore on, I surrendered to the pang of realizing that my life wasn't passing me by but rather spooling around me, churning in idleness.

"What's wrong?" Milton asked, offering the tea towel to dry my eyes.

"I don't know who I am," I said.

"Well," he replied, "who do you think you are?"

I flip through the collection to make sure its pages aren't highlighted by some overeager undergrad. To the shepherd, I read the line, "The constant happiness is curiosity."

The shepherd says, "Think of the cats, Alice; think of what husks off each of their nine lives."

I'd got her from the SPCA, and her history is a dead language. There's a DNA test you can send for, but I don't want to chase away her infinite possibilities. When she was a puppy, we would curl in bed, and I would whisper her name into her ear, again and again. It wasn't just so she could learn my voice, but I wanted to bring her joy, the toe-curling pleasure of being seen.

How much do I love him? Sometimes, when he's in the shower, I x-ray through his skin. And at each layer, I ask myself: these muscles, do I love them? These innards? These bones?

The answer is always the same.

I have read Milton's book—though you'd never know by how little I talk about it. It's a nonfiction called *Liable at Heart* (*La faute du cœur*) about how five years ago, Milton was engaged to a man named Edgar. The two were going to dinner where Milton was planning to call off the wedding. To avoid a scene, he chose a crowded downtown restaurant. Edgar was driving, accelerated through a yellow, and plowed into a left-turning Mustang.

The Mustang driver walked away unscathed, the right half of his vehicle squished up flush as if it were never there to begin with. But Edgar and Milton were rushed to the ER.

Milton's brain was swelling like a mushroom cloud, so in order to avoid permanent damage, the surgeon performed a decompressive craniectomy, which is where they uncork a circle of skull to let the brain swell through. If all goes well, they replace the bone in a few weeks with that smug satisfaction of a puzzle piece in its rightful spot. But in the meantime, between sawing and then sewing the skull, the patient carries the bit of bone around. The doctor stored it in Milton's inner thigh, deep in the fat, where it would stay safe and shining until needed again.

This took two months, start to finish. Two months and he's healed, and all that's left is a scar on his inner thigh, a white line the size of lips pursing at the mundane miracle of modern medicine.

But Edgar never recovers. He goes from spinal injury to encephalitis to sepsis to pneumonia. All the while, Milton stays with him. He reads to him, shaves him, feeds him from disposable spoons. And with every paragraph, every nicked chin, every half cup of apple sauce, Milton feels his heart swell like his brain once did.

It was a full year before Edgar's body finally buckled, a year's worth of penance for the right half of the Mustang.

The book ends with Milton taking a cab to Edgar's funeral. He writes that perhaps Edgar's death was merciful, because as the weeks turned into months and the months neared a year, Milton had sunk more and more in love, and if Edgar had lived even a day longer, it would've been unbearable to lose him. And so now, Milton will stay submerged at this neutral buoyancy for the rest of his life, deep enough to never ascend but shallow enough to still see the sunlight.

Beneath the Arc de Triomphe, I watched the whirlpool of vehicles. My guidebook said the traffic circle sees so many collisions that insurance companies no longer bother trying to find out who holds fault, the damage a de facto 50/50 split. Our daily dilemmas, whether we move too quickly or linger too long, trying to open ourselves to all that whirlpools around us.

When you look at rush hour from a distance, it's a miracle any of us are still alive. All thanks to our make-believe barriers:

the double solid lines, the two-second distance. But what's even more amazing—awe-inspiring, actually—is the total faith we put in strangers to not pop the bubbles between vehicles, strangers who we'll never meet or love but still trust as we do our sixteen-year-old dogsitters.

A couple of months ago, while Milton was out with friends, I was cleaning our apartment. In a gym bag of old clothes, I found the hockey helmet he wore when his skull was perforated. I put it on and, surprised that it fit, hit my head against the hardwood a good four or five times—just to see if it worked.

When I looked up, the shepherd was watching me. It was then that I first noticed her eyes had become white suns.

I was in the bathtub at Jen's apartment when my laptop dinged from the bedroom. I had emailed Milton pictures of me at the Roman crypts, the Champs-Élysées, the Canadian embassy; I'd also forwarded any newspaper articles that referenced his readings (even though I'm sure he'd already bookmarked them). None of this had been responded to.

I scrambled out of the tub and tapped my space bar to wake my computer.

I had given her my email after she drew the map. That was four days ago, and this was the first I'd heard. « Quelquels amis et moi allons boire un verre ce soir. Tu peux venir si tu vuex. »

In the bar, my hair still damp with bath water, I shook hands with her friends: Caroline, Eveline, and Micheline.

"From Canada?" Caroline said. "You must speak French."

Micheline leaned in. « Qu'est-ce que tu as fait aujourd'hui? »

I drained my wine to raise the courage. « Aujourd'hui, j'ai marché au église Saint Denis. »

« Et pourquoi est il un saint? » Micheline said, licking the red off her teeth.

« Parce que son tête étais couper. » I karate-chopped my neck. « Mais il l'ai retrouvé et il a marché away. »

Eveline asked, « Y a-t-il des saints au Canada? »

Up until this point, she'd shown no interest in the conversation. But with Eveline's question, she looked up from peeling her label. "They are all saints in Canada."

As the night unravelled, I admitted how much more I liked myself in French. When someone spoke with me, I hung off every sound, scrambling for a toehold word, my eyes riveted to the speaker, scouring their actions for the slightest movement—a flicker in the eyebrow, a curling of the lip—every twitch a breadcrumb; and when I was able to follow the story, how much shock I found in the narrative's turn, or tragedy in its pathos, or unfettered glee in its punchline.

Last call and I settled our bill. She took me to her apartment. Nobody had seen the tiger for days, nights. "It was the act of God," she told me. "God wanted the tiger to again be free."

Afterwards, on my way back to Jen's, I cut across a cemetery, past the graffitied graves, adorned with bubblegum, red lipstick, and cigarette butts.

Do I need to explain the feeling that you're being watched, that understanding when a pair of night-vision eyes has anchored onto you? Do I need to explain that crackling terror of feeling your fate being weighed and that secret thanks of knowing the end has finally arrived?

The shepherd says, "Did you think of me?"

I say, "I thought of you all the time."

"Like when?"

"Like the time I passed by the Le Tour Eiffel at dusk, and its searchlight swooped through the city."

The shepherd says, "Confess to me your greatest fear."

I say, "That I will never be brave enough to command my butterfly wings to cut through my caterpillar skin."

The shepherd says, "You've thought about this before."

I say, "Tell me yours."

"That we will one day catch what we have been chasing."

Her breath lengthens. I watch the rise and fall of her chest, each beat a bit longer.

I say, "Are you awake?"

And I confess what I'm really afraid of. I am afraid of what I want: for her to slip into a sleep that is bottomless.

The shepherd does not stir. She has gone deaf and no longer hears whispers.

We met on the internet, and after I picked him up, he navigated me to a drive-in an hour outside of Winnipeg. I forget the movie but remember it was screened against an old grain elevator. On the way home, we stopped for gas, and after I paid, I found him in the back of the store, hunched over a glass case. Inside and laid flat: the painting of dogs playing poker.

"What I wouldn't give," he said, "to see the original."

"Did I tell you I have a dog?" I asked.

His fingers fanned across the glass. "Can I buy this for him?"

"Her," I said.

"Oh," he said. "Even better."

Why is it that when we lose one thing, our instinct is to lose everything?

"Do you want money?" I asked.

She smiled and handed me my T-shirt. "Because you hope that will be easier?"

"Do you want," I said, struggling to find the word, "quelque chose?"

She collapsed onto the mattress and leaned her head against the pillow. Outside, night had risen, and the city shimmered like a tangled fishnet that we were caught within.

"I want," she said, chewing a fingernail, "to touch that tiger."

What a world we live in. That morning, you can be balancing on the handrail of the Esplanade Riel and all you need to do is sit with yourself in a fuselage for twelve hours, scream through some cerulean, and come evening you're strolling the laneways of a landlocked city whose emblem is a ship. *Fluctuat nec mergitur.* "Tossed but never sunk."

There are times when I, too, want to be battered and tossed, to have a rogue wave—like a rogue thought—haul me overboard as I plummet into the unknown, the water closing around me like a grave, darker and darker, unto pure gravity; but then, kicking wildly, I thrash and ascend, gasp at the surface as light returns and everything shines vivid and true: all so I could learn how to let go of a handrail, for holding on comes easily.

But then there are other times, like when I was cutting across the Pont des Arts and watched a shell game: three coconut halves and a ping-pong ball. For over an hour, the dealer courted passing tourists, letting them win a couple of rounds, until on the third or fourth, they pointed to the middle shell with such confidence that they bet it all and uncovered nothing. Oddly enough, after the con had been pulled, the dealer never had to tell his targets to leave and make room for the next mark. Rather, they left of their own accord, retreating with their credulity. Though one time, in a moment of inexplicable beauty, a backpacker gambled again, aware of the sleight of hand but betting on having it beat. But before the result was shown, the rollerblade gendarme arrived and scattered everyone like a dog flushing a flock of geese.

So many wrongs and so many rights, and the bureaucracy of saints keeping ticky-tacky track. But it's a doubtful line between martyr and moron, between divine sight and rose tint. When to give in to the undertow and when to white-knuckle the world?

"But really, it's all the same story: The body breaks, the body heals, but never fast enough. What did Edgar and I have? Something that existed beyond words—not just in the sense that words escape me (which they do), but in the sense that what we had existed above the confines of meaning; what we had existed in the sharp corners of the hospital room, in the ribbon of pitch from the monitor, in the long arms of dusk that wrapped themselves around the ICU; what we had, in that sense, was meaning-less." (*Liable at Heart*, 192)

The Persian rug has darkened, and the shepherd is whimpering. I scamper to the drawer, take out the emergency tea towels, and start soaking the puddle.

"Do you need a hand?" a customer offers.

"Shut your eyes," I hiss at him. "Pretend you don't know."

The shepherd whines, and I take her into my arms, turn us towards the do-gooder now browsing the poetry section. I say, "See, baby? Nobody saw. Nobody saw."

Mr Samaritan waits for five minutes, buys *The Circle Game* out of pity, and leaves. The bookstore grows cavernous.

The shepherd says, "Don't think I didn't spot the ruse. Nobody browses poetry."

"I've been meaning to ask," I say. "When you're asleep and your paws are shuffling, what are you dreaming about?"

She says, "All the things I would do if I had thumbs."

And just like that, quick as sin, she has forgiven herself.

Eight days in, I ran out of money. I emailed Milton and asked him to send a couple hundred. He responded immediately, saying nothing, but transferring $10,000, and is it an honest mistake or a settling of accounts? The password hint was, "name of my book," and I responded, "Self-Absorbed Yet Porous: The Autobiography of a Sponge" followed by "Boning on the Brain" until I remembered you can only fuck around twice before you lose it all.

Such small things can derail your year: the first time the dog can't jump onto the bed, a hand burrowing into the blankets when you reach for it. But isn't it incredible how long a tea-spoon of beauty can last you? Lifetimes, if you're lucky. Take Paris's oldest church: the two-dimensional frescoes, the smell of old stone, the footsteps sounding off the walls like water dripping from a distance; and then Mass started and you wer-en't ready to leave so you joined in—stood when everyone stood, sat when everyone sat, no one to know your falsehoods; and then as the priest (wearing a neck brace!) rose to offer the Eucharist, a man rushed down the aisle, waving a picket sign (*l'homosexualité est l'amour pas le péché*) and a church-goer in the front row (sitting where Milton, at his nephew's baptism, called the Splash Zone) raised a chair and exploded it off the protestor's back, the splinters confettying, all the while the ramrod priest stayed locked in his Latin chant, blessing our world; and in the time it took the man's body to crumple to the floor, you already knew that no one would ever hear this story, because you'd never be able to tell it, never be able to convey how much it meant to you: the Eucharist, the neck brace, your gasp as the wood turned into sawdust that hung in the candlelight before showering upon the face of the supine protestor, and he opened his mouth as if tasting snow.

Is it so bad to let slip just a little bit of suffering out of you into somebody else? Isn't it natural? Isn't it the law of energy?

Scraps of rat carcasses had been found along a side street, punctuated by the lacerated body of a raccoon. Later that day, signs hung from the balconies: *Rendez notre ville propre! Laissez le tigre vivre.*

We were supposed to meet at the terminal: Paris to Winnipeg, via Chicago. I arrived two hours early and watched the repeating fifteen minutes of security camera footage of the big cat skulking across a parking lot, licking some salt off the asphalt, before disappearing beyond the frame.

Then, they were preboarding, and then zones one and two, then three through five, and then it was final call, and mine and Milton's names were summoned to the desk and I was told it was now or never, and I searched for my seat, trying to delay takeoff, but the attendants cleared the aisles, shut the overhead compartments, and told a woman to upright her tray, and I couldn't stop staring at the heavy door when it began to roll closed like an eclipse.

But does he get on the plane?

I had given myself a paper cut with the boarding pass, so I ask the shepherd to lick the wound. My one souvenir, but how long before I heal and forget?

I say, "Do you ever think about each person in the world whom we haven't yet met but are nonetheless destined to love?"

The shepherd stops licking, says, "I told you that."

The mailman delivers a London Bridge postcard, addressed to Milton. On the back, someone named Stewart writes how lovely their conversation had been and how thankful he was to have read the book and how Milton expressed something within him that he'd known was there but was never sure how to uncover. "Remember to keep something for yourself," he writes, and then signs off with "See you soon!" and I'm not sure if that's wishful thinking or a done deal.

The tiger was shot at the dead-end of an alley. The front-pages ran a picture of her body, spotlit by the circle of a policeman's flashlight, crumpled among blossoming weeds, a trickle of blood from her black lips. Already, bouquets and chocolates have appeared, along with dead rats purchased from pets stores. There's a certain respect you've got to have for something that sticks around so long where it obviously shouldn't. And it occurs to me now that those passengers who stampeded out of the subway station may have been doing so under the belief that they were not running from the great beast but towards it.

Milton comes downstairs, and I shove the postcard into my back pocket.

"Do you want doughnuts?" he asks, and I nod as he kisses that muscle connecting my neck and shoulder blade.

He leaves, jay-walking across the street. He's started writing a new book but won't tell me what it's about.

I slip the postcard out of my pocket and with it comes a hand-drawn map of the face of a city. I file both into a copy of *Settlers of the Marsh*. Let some lost soul find these treasures in a hundred years.

The shepherd says, "I know a joke."

I say, "Let's hear it."

She says, "After Eden, Adam and Eve said to God, 'We are so alone.' So God created man's best friend. Adam and Eve left, and the Devil said to God, 'I thought you were still mad at them.' And God said, 'Oh, I am. Let me tell you about a little something called Dog Years.'"

I lower myself to all fours and touch our cheeks together. I say, "I thought you'd die without me."

She says, "I know."

I say, "That's the only reason I left."

She says, "I know."

The sleigh bells herald Milton's return. I stand as he hands me a still-warm doughnut. Our fingers overlap, and for a blink, he and I are wrist over wrist, as dawn spills across the washed-out white of airplane wing.

When he's in the shower, and I am x-raying through him, I can see the puzzle piece in his skull, that chunk of light safely stapled where it needs to be. And I love it. I love how it waited and waited, ready for him to heal, ready for our fates to be decided.

"Your thumb is bleeding," he says, kissing the cut.

I have picked the scab.

GRAVITY

Killing time before it got dark, we were going to see the advanced screening of *The Nativity Story* since it's rumoured to have a breastfeeding scene. But Levi Henders, the theatre's assistant manager, said Patrick's been banned for life because he was caught masturbating to *March of the Penguins*. Patrick swore it had nothing to do with the tuxedo birds or the grandeur of their Antarctic habitat but that he was so inconceivably bored. Levi corrected himself and said, "masturbating during *March of the Penguins*," but a ban is still a ban.

"Fuck this, Danny," Patrick said and then spat on Levi's dress shoes. "Let's go make some pastries."

So we're in the abandoned lot, the one beside the post office, in Patrick's '91 Dodge Ram, squealing doughnuts across the weedy asphalt. Patrick is driving, and I've rolled down the window, letting the force swing my face out of the cab. Patrick starts doing his impression of Levi, hollering over the tires, "Hands in the popcorn, not in your pants!"

The impersonation is a party trick, something everyone wants to see and something Patrick loves to give. It's hard to do it justice, but it's Academy-level acting: the nasal drawl, impeccable; the subtle slur, flawless; the puffed out and crooked bottom lip, sublime. He even gets Levi's bum arm right, dangling from the socket, really capturing his inner struggle. I start to laugh and soon it's hard to breathe.

"That's not what the napkins are for!"

My left hand is clamped onto the armrest to keep me from being sucked out the window, and the wind is thrilling against my face. Patrick stomps on the e-brake and the back tires burn so bad that we twirl into their smoke and the smell hits the back of the mouth.

He lets his foot off the gas, the truck slams into stillness, and the air begins to clear.

"What's the time?" Patrick asks, his voice now flat. The car radio is always flashing midnight. I check my watch. "Nine-fifteen."

Patrick opens his door and the truck frantically dings because he's left the engine idling. He jogs around the hood, then reaches through my open window to pull up my door lock. "You're driving," he says. "Time to get to work."

I shuffle over to the driver's seat while Patrick takes shotgun. I twist the key in the ignition but since it's already running, the engine screams, shrill as pain.

Woodside has been our town's mayor for the past twenty-six years—Ms Haxton says that's two years longer than Saddam led Iraq. For the past four elections, he's run uncontested. This time, not only does he have an opponent—Dr Gregory "Call-Me-Greg" Gibbs—but he's losing. Bad. At least, he was until yesterday. Forty-eight hours before the polls opened, our town newsletter broke that Gibbs was cheating on his wife with Olivia who runs Olivia and Paul's Outdoor Paintball. It was the biggest story the newsletter ran since Sandra Schmirler came in '95 to cut the ribbon for the rink.

Gibbs moved here seven years ago when the federal government was forgiving student loans if you worked in a shithole for half a decade. After her first ultrasound, Janny asked him why he stayed, and he said it was because he loved the open spaces. All those endless haystacks, pocked with bullet wounds of paint.

Patrick pulls out a mickey of whiskey from under the seat. He takes a swig, the liquid gurgling through the bottle's neck and sloshing back. He hands me the bottle and I down as much as I can stomach.

From the glove box, he grabs five different colour pills. He calls it his "granola." "Danny, which one you want?"

Janny asked me to stop popping pills when the baby's around, and I hastily agreed because I didn't want her to think I'm not ready to be a father. "Parenting is all about sacrifice," she keeps saying. But I'm not sure if it counts when the baby's still in her belly. But Janny and her belly aren't here now. I think she's still out of town for a couple days.

I take the pink pill from Patrick's hand, its capsule dewy with sweat, and palm it into my mouth. The sun sinks so early these days. And there never seems to be a moon.

Patrick takes back the bottle and says that when we're finished, I can spend the night at his house so I don't have to walk home. I was hoping he'd just offer me a ride. His house always smells like cat piss even though he doesn't own a cat, and Emily's always there and we've never really got along because she's always wanting me to touch her. But I can't think of a polite reason to say no.

Gibbs is running on the promise that he'll resist amalgamation with Calgary, refusing to become a subdivision of the sprawl. Woodside argues it'll be good for us but everyone knows his hands are dirty. Gibbs says that if we amalgamate, we won't be able to choose our future—rich folks will come and bulldoze Schmirler's rink into a Toyota dealership. In its last poll, the newsletter had Gibbs thirty-six points ahead. But then Paintgate happened.

The good doctor's got a bunch of money and has put campaign signs a good fifty kilometres beyond the town's western limits, posting on both sides of the road, right up to the big city's border. We drive west on the open highway, waiting to pass the last sign. Each time we think we've reached the final one, we see the glossy shine of the headlights against another three kilometres down.

I feel the pill surging through my body, turning my pulse into firecrackers. The telephone poles whip past us like hiccups and I can see my heartbeat in my eyes. Through the seat I can feel Patrick's knees jostling. "If we're caught," he says, "you can't stop me from ratting out Woodside."

"Say whatever you want, Patty-Cakes. It's a free country."

Calgary's yellow dome of light blooms from the horizon, blotting out the galaxies above. Last year, for her fifteenth, I got Janny two tickets to see the Flames play Dallas. Three rows behind the penalty box. It took us two hours to hitchhike into the city and then a dollar-fifty each for the bus downtown. When we finally got to the Saddledome, there was a guy at the door wanting to buy tickets. Ours had cost $120 each, but he offered us $350 for both. We didn't talk much on the long hitch home, but I bet she appreciates the extra money now. Parenting is all about sacrifice.

"I think that was the last one," Patrick says, craning his neck to look behind him. I don't see anything ahead, so I swing a U-turn and we each take a permanent marker from the cup holder. I park the truck and jog across the road to get one of the signs. I pull Mayor Woodside's note from my pocket and shine my keychain flashlight on it. The handwritten list has all of Gibbs's campaign signs that we're supposed to graffiti.

"What does yours say?" I holler to Patrick.

"It's got a picture of Ron Trest—that guy from the grocery store—saying, 'I've trusted Greg with my life.' He's giving a thumbs-up."

Gibbs did this thing where he had his patients saying what a bang-up guy he is.

"Okay," I say, dragging my thumb down the list until I see Ron's name. "Leave it here and change 'life' to 'wife'."

My sign has a picture of Susan Lane from the flower shop saying, "Greg cares." Susan's not on the list so I toss her into the flatbed. Whatever's not on the list, we're supposed to burn.

I get back to the truck before Patrick does, so I sit shotgun. The overhead light clicks off. Through the windshield, Patrick's cigarette pulses like a lighthouse. I down some whiskey and my head gathers mass like a dying star.

The night runs slow and long, the flatbed gradually filling. After each stop, we switch shotgun and driver. Patrick lets the engine idle, but I'm respectful of the environment so I kill it. Besides, when the headlights fade, the black is so thick I pretend I'm walking on the outer planets, where the sun can't reach, and I breathe like Darth Vader and my flashlight on a rock is the glow of alien eyes. The clouds of galaxies circle their bodies above me. And out here, in silty space, it's just me and this vacuum of silence, the suction of solar winds and a sign with Ruth Merwin from the gas station that says, "Greg will fix things."

I consult the list, change "fix" to "fuck," and head back to the truck.

We take two hours for the western outskirts.

The whiskey's gone so Patrick pulls into the liquor store. Travis Stenton is standing behind the cash wearing his eyepatch and reading *Hustler*. He looks up at us as Patrick walks to the whiskey aisle.

"Danny, how's Janny doing?" Travis asks.

"Good," I say. "Thanks for asking."

"Do you know if it's a boy or girl?"

"We don't want to know. If it's a boy we're thinking of naming him Randy, after my grandfather—the one who raised me. If it's a girl, I'd like to name her Janet after her mommy."

"Danny, Janny, and Randy or Janny. You guys could start a folk band."

"How's the eye?" I ask.

"Still lazy. Gibbs says I have to work it more." He holds up his magazine. "So this is prescribed."

Patrick comes to the till with another mickey and I peel off one of Woodside's twenties. Travis takes the money and smiles, "You boys have a safe night."

Outside the liquor store, Patrick twists the cap and passes me the bottle. He takes out his granola and hands me a purple. I take a sip for the pill and pass the bottle back to him, but he's swallowed it dry.

We ricochet down the roads, changing Wayne Thorton's "Greg loves this town" to "Greg loves to get blown" or adding the word "job" to the end of Linda Sherbrook's "Greg will give this city a hand."

When we've got them all, the flatbed heaped, Patrick says he needs to jet home to pick up another pack of smokes and make sure Emily's okay. He parks around back, and I follow him onto his porch and take a seat on one of his lawn chairs. He goes in and I listen to Emily panic with excitement. He doesn't know it but I can hear him through the door, speaking in this baby voice. "I wuv you, too. I wuv you, too."

I get up and peer through the blinds. Emily is cuddled onto Patrick's lap, his arms wrapped around her neck with his ear pressed against her chest.

Patrick and his mom moved here from Calgary eight years ago. The only thing Patrick has ever told me about his father was that he's a "bad, bad man." We've been best friends since grade five. A year ago, after his mother hung herself with a plugged-in strand of Christmas lights, Patrick became the youngest person in town to own a house. The city clerk, Charity Knowles, said he couldn't take the deed because he was only sixteen, but then Patrick said he was actually eighteen, proving it with a creased-up birth-certificate, and that he'd been lying ever since he got here because he'd been held back two years but didn't want people to think he was stupid. "Who's stupid now?" he kept asking Charity before the public works guys told him to leave.

"I wuv you, too. I wuv you, too."

I sit back down. Above my lawn chair, there's a porch light that works on a motion detector. It switches off in stillness so I keep waving it awake. But after the third or fourth time, I decide to let it stay dark.

God, I'm going to love that kid so much.

I think I've found Orion's Belt because it's just three stars in a row. But Orion seems to have a lot of belts.

• • •

Janny is walking towards me. At first, it's just her silhouette since she's backlit by headlights, but I recognize the bump. She comes so close I feel her breath on my skin. Her eyes are raw and red, like she was crying and crying until she dried up. She takes my hand and brings it against her stomach. I'm hoping she wants me to feel it kick, but her belly's still as snow. She starts sliding my hand down until she's pressed both our palms against her groin and I can feel the wetness through her dress.

I jolt awake to Patrick sinking my hand into a bowl of ice.

He's swallowing his laughter, and I kick him in the shin. "It needs to be hot water, you fucking orphan."

I hear Emily somewhere behind the raspberry bushes. Patrick tosses the bowl onto the grass and I follow him to the truck.

"You're driving," he says and throws the keys blindly over his shoulder towards me. "And shut the gate behind you."

"How 'bout I shut your fucking throat?"

There is a small forest a couple clicks east. Leading away from Calgary, there's no commuters going this direction, so the road doesn't boast a single sign for either candidate.

Patrick takes a gulp of whiskey. He holds onto the bottle. "Have you ever thought that if your mom and you were the same age, and she wasn't your mom, would you be friends?"

Lately he's started asking me all these hypotheticals about my mother—a woman I'd only met a handful of times—and it's getting dull.

"No," I say.

"No, you wouldn't be friends?"

"No, I have never thought about it."

I scroll through the radio, but it's only static.

"Yeah, I think my mom and I would've," he says. "I hear that before she had me, she was really into cars and thinking of opening an auto shop."

I can't picture Patrick's mother in any outfit other than her 7-Eleven uniform.

"Sometimes," he continues, "I think what if I hadn't finished the milk or hadn't put her cotton shirt in the dryer. Or if that blue jay hadn't flown into the window, or those cockroaches were a half-second quicker and got under the fridge before she'd seen them."

I check the radio again but it just hisses ghost music.

He takes a tight-lipped sip. "But then," he says, "sometimes it's the other way around and I'm like, What took you so long?" He takes another drink and passes me the bottle. "Do you think I'm responsible?" he asks.

I grab the whiskey, take a long drink, and wedge the bottle between my legs. "I think we're responsible for a lot of things that aren't our fault." And then the front left tire dips into a pothole and the whole truck is swallowed by the recoil.

I've spilled on myself. "Shit," I say, shoving the bottle at Patrick. "Look what you've done."

Before he can start talking again, I find CBC. The signal's weak and the announcer crackles when he says now is the national time signal. There are the three short tones and I strain my ear for the long dash that'll cue the top of the hour, but the signal has died.

I veer us off the highway and onto a dirt road. The headlights flicker between the trees and it begins to snow. At a swelling in the road, big enough for us to turn around, I stop and twist off the engine.

Out of the cab, Patrick unlatches the tailgate and we scramble into the back of the flatbed and start kicking out the election signs. Once all the signs are heaped on the frozen mud, I have to piss so I walk into the woods as Patrick begins to glug a half-quart of engine oil onto the smiling faces of our fellow citizens.

The snow dresses the trees in white. Maybe I'll ask Janny to marry me when she gets back. The solstice isn't even here yet but I can't remember what summer was like. A pile of deer bones glistens with ice, sparkles like treasure.

When I get back to the vehicle, there's a churning pillar of smoke, tilting in the wind. And through the smoke I see it: the face of my child when it's my age. When he is my age. Because it's a boy. Randy. And he's calling my name. "Danny. Danny. Danny." My son has put me in a trance. "Danny. Danny."

"Danny!" Patrick shouts from the other side of the fire. "This is good enough." He jogs back to the truck, blowing on his fists to keep warm, sits shotgun.

I stumble behind the wheel, steer us out of the forest and onto the paved road that lifts us onto its smooth back. I gag on a strand of hair in the back of my mouth and when I tongue it to my lips and pull, I feel the rest of it slither from between my molar and cheek. Must be one of Janny's.

It's been a long night, and we're staring at the dotted yellow line spinning beneath us. In the thick light of the headlights, the snow turns to stars as we travel at warp speed, combusting through galaxies.

Patrick offers me a smoke but my tummy's all twisty. He's burning through an entire pack, lighting the new ones with the butts of the old ones, something he calls "making the tips kiss." He's kept the window up so the smoke layers itself around us. He coughs and says something but the hearing in my right ear isn't great so I get him to repeat it. He holds the cigarette in front of his face. "I said, the things I love are killing me."

When I turn back to the highway, a shadow bolts from the ditch and is swallowed by the tires.

"What the fuck was that?" Patrick says, spinning his head back as I slam on the brakes.

In the rearview, there's a black heap on the yellow line. "I think it was a coyote."

"Lovely," Patrick says. "We can skin it for fur." He's out of the truck, running to the corpse.

At first, I think the coyote is still alive and is yelping to its pack for help. But as I get closer, I see that it is Patrick who's howling. I see a glint of metal.

A collar and a dog tag.

Emily.

Her body is so big and limp that her legs keep falling free from Patrick's arms. He's rocking her back and forth, "I'm so sorry, I'm so sorry. Oh god, sosorry, sosorrysosorry."

"How the fuck did she get out here?" I ask. But Patrick doesn't answer. Janny once told me that aliens probably don't exist because for all of the things a planet needs to sustain life, there's only, like, a one in a trillion chance of them ever lining up. What I'm getting at is that stranger stuff has happened but we find a way to accept it.

I head back to the truck, finish off the whiskey. The sky clears up then clouds up.

I think Janny is home tomorrow. I know I have it written on the fridge. I should get her a bouquet or something. If it was lighter out, I'd pick her some highway flowers. *To Janny, Some wild-flowers for your wild heart.* But I guess the winter has killed everything. And Susan Lane charges a fortune for a bouquet. I'll just make a card. It's all about sacrifices.

You'd think from Patrick's moans that it was him I'd hit. I went to his mother's funeral. After the closed-casket ceremony had finished, Patrick was a pallbearer. Dead-eyed the entire time.

Walking back to the bodies, I make my voice all gentle because I'm trying to respect the situation. "Patrick, look, it's just bad luck. Let's get her in the flatbed and we can go home and I'll help you bury her early tomorrow morning. Give her a good funeral."

"Fuck you!" he shouts, his face sopping wet with tears and snot.

"Patrick, buddy, let's go."

Patrick just keeps rocking her back and forth, apologizing and apologizing.

"Patrick, we have to go."

"Why, Danny? Why do we have to go? It's my truck. I don't have to go anywhere."

"Patrick," I say, "It's Wednesday night, Thursday by now. We have school tomorrow."

So here's Patrick kneeling in the middle of the road, the blood beginning to freeze to his coat, the truck idling behind him like some shivering mourner. And the snow continues to scatter.

"Patrick?"

He takes a big sniff of snot. "Yeah?"

"Can I have the last pill?"

"What?"

"The last pill. It's a really long walk. Can I have it?"

He doesn't do anything for a bit, just rocks Emily's body, her tongue lolling out. Then he looks up, and I'm startled by how raw his eyes are.

Patrick throws the pill across the tarmac, bouncing like a pebble. I don't say anything. I pull out Woodside's roll of twenties, rip Patrick's half from the elastic and throw it onto the road.

I hunch over and scour the road with my keychain flashlight until I find the pill, the red capsule like a drop of blood. I look up and there's Patty-Cakes watching me, hating me.

At first, I was going to pick up the pill. But I've changed my mind. Patrick so badly wants to see which of us has sunk further, and I want that to be a secret dug so deep even I don't know where it's buried. Besides, it might actually be just a drop of blood.

I start the walk home on this blacktop treadmill, Patrick's howls beginning again behind me. I toss the empty whiskey bottle over my shoulder and there's that sharp inhale of silence before it shatters.

God, I can't wait to hold that kid. Randy. Janny. Everything's going to be perfect then.

I can no longer tell what is star and what is snow. I shut that gate, didn't I?

Now that I think about it, maybe Janny is actually back this time *next* week. Whenever somebody says, "I'll be there next

Friday," I'm never sure if they mean the Friday coming up or the one after that.

· · ·

I trudge past town hall. Its clock says 3:20 but that thing's broken so often, who knows if it's right. I roll up my sleeve to find my wrist bare and tender. What happened to my watch?

Travis is outside the liquor store, heaving on a cigarette so hard I can hear the paper crinkle. He waves me over and his eyepatch has been flipped up onto his forehead.

"Where's Patrick?"

"He was beat," I say, "so I told him I'd walk. You done your shift?"

"Just about," Travis says, his bad eye sinks from my gaze to stare at the concrete. "Couple kids from Calgary drove in and robbed me. But I'd made a drop a few minutes earlier so they only got sixty bucks."

"They have a gun?"

"No," Travis says and begins to chuckle.

"A knife?"

"Almost." He's really trying to hold it back.

"A bat?"

He shakes his head in tight little jitters.

"Did they have anything?"

"A sword!" he says, busting a gut.

"A sword?"

"A motherfucking sword."

Travis acts out a couple moves, swooshing his hands. And I start laughing with him. Really letting myself go. We lean in, holding each other up, laughing and laughing. This'll be what

I miss most when the kid comes, this infinite simplicity. But something is coming for us, dragging us.

We calm down, and there's that moment of beautiful silence. Travis asks, "If you were old enough, who'd you vote for?"

"No one," I say, wiping my nose with my sleeve. "I don't believe in democracy."

SEA CHANGE

They had known each other for five hours—but it was, mind you, five hours straight—when Rebecca stopped fidgeting with her coaster, leaned across the table, and asked Lee, "What do you think about having an affair?"

"Like," Lee said, "in general, or with...?"

"With me," Rebecca said.

The server arrived with the mojitos Rebecca had ordered before she sat down.

"Two more," she said to the server, who nodded and cleared away their empty plates.

"But we have to go soon," said Lee.

Rebecca shrugged. "It's an all-inclusive. Worst-case scenario, you throw them out."

But here, in the Club Cubaño Seafood Buffet, among the potted palm trees and ladder-back chairs, Lee knew that, in the shadow of Rebecca's question, the worst-case scenario was not that the drinks would arrive tardy and be left untouched. Rather, the worst-case scenario was that the drinks would arrive promptly and be touched until they were empty and he was honest.

The server finished wiping the table, and Lee offered her a twenty-peso bill, which she waved off and left.

"So," Rebecca said, leaning further, "what do you think?"

"What do *I* think?" Lee echoed. It wasn't that he wanted to say no; it wasn't that he wanted to say yes, either. He didn't know what he wanted but knew his answer would echo in his life for a long, long time. He chewed his lip and repeated the question, testing it out with different stresses. "What *do* I think? What do I *think*?"

"Yeah," said Rebecca, slouching into her chair. "Me too."

She watched the last of the lunch crowd exit the buffet and disperse into the white tile lobby. On the lobby's north-facing wall was an enormous mural, nine metres tall by seventy metres wide. It had been painted in the blocky, modernist style of Diego Rivera, but instead of displaying the violent and torquing progression of the proletariat into the bright light of self-realization, the mural showed the many (many!) activities that guests could enjoy with the simple act of existence.

At the painting's base, square-shaped bodies (all of whom were white) wrestled and frolicked in the sand, while above them, guests in a thatched roof gazebo danced the limbo and drank from coconut shells. On the wings, men and women surfed through tunnelling waves and water-skied amongst leaping dolphins. Cigars were smoked, roulette wheels spun, and dinner plates pyramided high with meat. But overtop it all, reclined a single person, stretched as long and sexless as an angel, in a linen robe by the side of a pool. There, in the aquamarine, was the resort's motto: *Freely We Serve, Because Freely We Love.*

"Well," Rebecca said, ripping her coaster in half, "we've got three days to decide."

"We should go," Lee said, standing up. The afternoon's panel was starting soon, and the longer they lingered, the more likely the mojitos would arrive.

This was the first British Columbia Teachers' Union Pedagogical Conference (TUP-C) since the pandemic three years prior. Having the funds from those cancelled conferences sitting in a high-interest (though ethically dubious) investment portfolio, there was consensus on the executive committee that this year's location should be far more momentous than Castlegar or Salmon Arm. Indeed, nowhere in the province seemed up to the glitz that the situation demanded; Vancouver, perhaps—but since 75 percent of the province's teachers (including Rebecca) already worked in the Greater Vancouver Area, a long weekend at Richmond's River Rock Casino was hardly considered exotic. Furthermore, since it was in the union's constitution to host their conferences solely at unionized hotels, and the swankiest venues in any city were all owned by ruthless corporations, that left only the most mundane, the most local of options.

These are the reasons that brought both Rebecca (a high school outdoor education teacher and guidance counsellor) and Lee (a grade seven mathematics and choir teacher) to the Camilo Cienfuegos conference room in the Atlantic Adventure All-Inclusive Resort, located forty-five minutes east of Havana, Cuba. The resort was both affordable yet extravagant and, technically speaking, was unionized to the strictest of international standards.

They had met in the lineup at the front desk, arriving simultaneously, and Lee said, "M'lady," and let her go first. But he was unsure if Rebecca remembered this meet-cute because she was so transfixed by the lobby's mural as the morning sun cathedralled through the wall of windows and bathed the scene in soft light. Lee, knowing he was in the presence of Art, took a photo on his phone.

Their first real introduction, however, was a half-hour later, after the two had left their bags in their respective rooms and the Welcome Address by Union President Orianna Nast had concluded. Lee was at the Shade Grown Coffee Bar, rigid at the counter, waiting to be helped as every teacher from the four corners of the province was served before him. The day's first seminar, The Building Blocks of Deconstruction, was starting in twenty minutes.

"You've got to lean," Rebecca said, beside him. "Over the bar."

She did so, flagging down the barista, and Lee noted the heft of her hips against the counter, the squeeze of her khakis around her thighs.

She uprighted and asked Lee what he wanted.

"An Americano," he said, and then in a whisper asked, "or is that insensitive?"

"Two Americanos," she told the barista, and then added "with Baileys," because she had caught Lee staring.

Not every teacher in the province attended TUP-C. Each district was allowed a set number of invitations, for which teachers had to apply to their local's executive. The conference, however, always took place at the tail-end of summer, as the impending school year gathered on the horizon like a tsunami, dark and fast-moving, and most districts had more invitations than applicants. Furthermore, there was also the shocking number of anti-vaxxers (pre-dominantly located in the Kootenays) who were barred from air travel. All told, around nine hundred teachers checked in to the Atlantic Adventure.

But because health regulations had weeded out the infected and impure, in addition to the union booking every room, the resort was able to allow a mask-free policy. As Lee waited with Rebecca at the Shade Grown Coffee Bar, he stared at the unobstructed faces of the crowd—the plump of the lips, the carnality of the teeth—and the room became imbued with an intimate yet pornographic feel: that something flagrant and liberating, impulsive and bohemian, could happen at any moment.

Many teachers had arrived a day or two earlier, but both Lee and Rebecca had flown the red-eye from Vancouver via Montreal that morning. The shuttle from the Juan Gualberto Gómez Airport, which served several resorts and hotels, was standing-room only because the previous shuttle had been cancelled due to a spate of pro-democracy protests in Havana.

Overtop the hiss of the espresso machine, Lee asked Rebecca if she had been to an all-inclusive before.

"Not in Cuba," she said, "but my husband and I go to one every other year."

This was the first mention of Rebecca's husband, and Lee was surprised to feel himself disappointed.

"Where have you gone?" he asked.

"Guatemala, Haiti, Liberia."

"So six years. You've been married six years."

"Quick math," said Rebecca.

"I'm a math teacher," said Lee, instantly regretting it. "And choir."

"Eight years, actually," said Rebecca. "We honeymooned at the Disney Resort in Orlando."

"Do you have kids?"

Rebecca said, "Why would we ever go there with kids? They'd ruin it."

"At those other places," Lee asked, "is the service always this…"

"Bad?" said Rebecca. "Terrible? Glacial?"

Lee nodded. It felt unfair to rag on people who were obviously poorer than him, but in this particular situation, surely they had more power—at least sociologically.

"Not always," said Rebecca. "But according to the travel books, it's par for the course here. Jobs are guaranteed by the state."

She didn't know if this last part was true but it certainly seemed it; and besides, in her experience, if you didn't start by explaining things to men, they'd start explaining things to you.

Lee watched a band teacher he knew (who had taken paid stress leave throughout the pandemic's months of online teaching) unwrap a complementary chocolate and, with neither hesitation nor shame, throw the wrapper on the floor.

Lee said, "I guess this is not the time to bemoan the pitfalls of job security."

In reality (meaning their lives outside the resort), both Lee and Rebecca were exceptional teachers. Lee, from Kamloops, ran his math class with charisma and chaos, so the students believed the equations were wild and spontaneous and that they themselves stood on the precipice of discovery. And for his choir class, he chose pop songs from contemporary musicals that featured spoken-word interludes, meaning that even his tone-deaf students could have a solo. He knew nothing about fine art but accepted his principal's suggestion he take the job simply because he loved to sing and hear people sing.

And Rebecca, from Vancouver (Burnaby, actually), was a once-in-a-generation talent. Seven years ago, she had won the inaugural Gaudreau award for "bringing the construct of the classroom into the sunlight, figuratively and literally." The prestigious award was sponsored by HG Energy and Minerals and came with a ten-thousand-dollar cheque for the winner, who was chosen based upon anonymous student letters of support. When Rebecca heard she had been nominated, she launched a covert campaign to discover which former students had championed her, and she retroactively changed their grades to As. She was overwhelmed with gratitude but couldn't think of any other way to repay or even articulate it. (At times, this had also been a problem in her marriage.) When she had won, the provincial arm of the national broadcaster reported on it, and every time she now met a fellow teacher, she had the slightly narcissistic yet remarkably vulnerable thought of, "I wonder if they know me."

The barista arrived with their Americanos.

"Muchos gracias," Lee said and offered him a ten-peso bill, which was accepted with a slow blink of insouciance. Lee assumed the barista's dispassion was from having grown up in the vestiges of Stalinist Communism, where even smiles were regulated. "Be free," Lee wanted to tell him. "Let your heart sing." (This, of course, was what he told the lock-jawed tweens of his choir.)

"You know," said Rebecca, "it's not expected you tip."

"That's why I'm doing it," said Lee, tucking his wallet back into his chinos. "In a couple of days, word'll get around about the generous man from Kamloops, and while you're all climbing over each other to get a sandwich, I'll have the world at a beckon."

Rebecca nodded and let a moment pass where she watched his boyish charm of believing he had it all figured out. The moment faded.

"You know they have to tip out, right?"

"Tip out?"

"Anything you give them is split up by the entire staff. Look at their pant pockets. They're sewn shut so they can't hide money. Your ten pesos is divided by, like, two thousand. So that's what? A cent?"

It was, Lee knew, half a cent. And it was, Rebecca knew, not called a cent but a centavo.

At the last TUP-C, three years ago at the Vancouver Island Conference Centre and Hotel in Nanaimo, the seminar Gamifying Your Classroom (sponsored by Ubisoft) was scheduled at the same time as Decolonizing the Report Card. The Gamifying conference room was filled past fire code, while a social studies teacher from Whistler tweeted out a photo of the desolate Decolonizing room (#WhoTeachesTheTeachers?), and the union had to pay 15K to a crisis management firm to weather the storm.

One of the policy changes this year was that seminars and panels were no longer scheduled to compete with each other but were organized single file throughout the (very long) day. Teachers used to be expected to attend an event in each of the day's three blocks. Now, however, because the days were expanded to six blocks (two seminars after breakfast, two panels after lunch, two lectures after dinner) and the time commitment of going to all of them exceeded union standards, teachers weren't expected to attend a set number but just as many as they reasonably could.

"You have options!" the welcome pamphlet proclaimed. "And how you take advantage of them is up to you."

The difference in size between the audience for the Welcome Address by Union President Orianna Nast and the opening workshop, Bridges Over Walls: An Inclusive Classroom, foretold the future of this optional attendance. As opposed to the Welcome Address's filled room of eight hundred seats, the same room now held only one hundred people, a number of attendees that the slam poetry open mic Rebecca frequented (but never read at) would have absolutely killed for, but in the gargantuan Camilo Cienfuegos conference room, the crowd seemed anaemic.

"My god," Lee whispered to Rebecca. "It looks like mass at the cathedral."

"You're Christian?"

"Me? God no," said Lee. "But my wife is."

The two filed to a pair of seats in the middle of the ocean of upholstery.

"What?" Lee said. "You seem disappointed."

After the seminar (which, despite the skeletal attendance, still set aside twenty-five minutes for Q and A), Lee and Rebecca got lunch at the Club Cubaño Seafood Buffet where Lee kept lavishly tipping the attendants, even though each gratuity was accepted with the same disenchantment.

"Are you going on any of the excursions?" Rebecca asked while cracking open her crab legs.

Each night, after the evening's final lecture, the union hired a fleet of buses to take any interested teachers to the UNESCO World Heritage site of Old Havana for various cultural activities.

"I'm thinking of doing the rum tasting," said Lee. "Maybe the Martyrs of the Revolution Ghost Tour. What about you?"

"I just like to walk."

Before leaving her home in Vancouver (Burnaby, actually), Rebecca had studied the online maps of Havana, tracking the sites she wished to see: the Capitol, the Grand Theatre, the National Hotel—all of them so fragile in their baroque perfection, it seemed a mystery how they survived a single day of revolution.

During the twilight of her undergraduate years, Rebecca had filled an elective with a Philosophy of Architecture class. She'd long since forgotten the majority of it (how many names did a column need?) but could still vividly recall the professor: a gentle, bald man who had a stomach so round and tympanic he seemed drafted by a compass. And he, perhaps knowing that his lectures were being poured into the sieve skulls of upperclassmen, would take every opportunity to remind them, "Architecture is the construction of fate." The idea, if Rebecca remembered correctly, was that true architecture is not simply drawing an ideal structure but rather designing an ideal world; because we, like water, form to the containers that hold us. In her mind, Rebecca's professor stood before his slide's projection of the Royal Salt Works in eastern France, his spherical form haloed by the factory's effortless symmetry, the equanimity of its outbuildings. His voice not his but the building's itself: "The art, therefore, is to imagine something that stands not isolated from time but moves within its currents and, as such, shall change our course."

Rebecca zoomed in and out of her online map, planning her routes, until she caught her eye on a building called *Sede Nacional Unión de Jóvenes Comunistas*, a name her app translated into the National Headquarters for Communist Youngsters. Their motto, according to the same app, was: "Study, Work, Rifle."

The edifice itself was boring—a concrete, thin-windowed tower painted beige. But there was something about the building that made Rebecca long to see it, how it so plainly stated exactly what it was.

Lee said, "I'd also love to smoke indoors. You know, for the novelty."

"It's cancelled."

This was not from Rebecca but from another lunch guest sitting beside them at the long table. Both Lee and Rebecca were startled by this interruption that wasn't really an interruption at all but merely a widening of the conversational circle. But the degree to which they jumped demonstrated how intimate they had become with each other's company, slowly sectioning themselves off from the world—a Cuba all their own.

"You haven't heard?" the man asked as he slurped an oyster off the half shell. He was wearing a visor (something Lee had only seen on professional tennis players), and his face was raccooned with a sunglass tan from having spent all morning pool-side.

He wiped his fingers on his bathing suit and extended his hand to Lee. "Josh Ribbins. Kelowna, 7/8 French."

But before Lee could introduce himself, Rebecca said, "Heard what?"

Monsieur Ribbins pulled his cell phone from his bathing suit's thigh pocket and started scrolling.

"Here," he said, passing the phone to Lee but which Rebecca accepted. She saw photos of streets choked with people, police kneeling on a woman's back, an antique Plymouth overturned and on fire. Lee scooched his chair around the table to sit beside her, reading over her shoulder, his chin inches above the rise of her bra strap beneath her blouse.

Monsieur Ribbins said, "All Havana's shut down."

Rebecca handed him back his phone, which he accepted and asked if they wished to join him that afternoon on the banana boat. "It's an inflatable tube that we sit on and get zipped behind a jet ski."

Lee and Rebecca declined, opting instead for the afternoon's two panel discussions—Methodologies for Qualitative and Differentiated Actions in Transformative Praxis; and WHIMIS. Monsieur Ribbins bid them au revoir (pronouncing each of the consonants) and left them alone at their end of the table. The entire cafeteria was emptying.

"Where's everyone going?" Lee asked. "The panel doesn't start for another thirty."

Rebecca checked her watch: 12:58. It had been nearly five hours since she ordered their Americanos. "The pool-side bar opens in two minutes."

"It makes me sad," said Lee, "that we won't get to see authentic Cuba."

"Look around," said Rebecca, gesturing to the decorative fishing poles, the roving mariachi band, the mural in the lobby. "This is authentic as it gets."

Over her shoulder, Lee saw a busboy carry a plastic bag of frozen crab legs, the label of which was in Chinese or Korean— Lee, from Kamloops, couldn't be expected to tell which was which.

Rebecca glanced at her watch again. It was now exactly five hours since they had met. She saw the server approaching with the two mojitos she'd ordered before sitting down. She stopped fidgeting with her coaster, leaned across the table, and asked, "What do you think about having an affair?"

Attendance continued to plummet. That evening—Rebecca's question still unanswered by either of them—the two spouses entered the Camilo Cienfuegos conference room to find the day's final lecture had been cancelled because the keynote speaker, a high school English teacher who had *taught a deaf teen how to speak*, was MIA.

Union President Orianna Nast stopped Lee and Rebecca at the door. "I saw her earlier today," Orianna Nast said, tucking her asymmetrical haircut behind her ear. "By the water slide. It must be a case of jet lag."

From the lobby, someone yelled, "Boob sweat."

Rebecca wondered if Orianna Nast remembered her from the Gaudreau award ceremony. Indeed, she was the one who had handed Rebecca the cheque. True, the Gaudreau had been awarded six times since then, and Rebecca herself didn't know any of the recipients, but there had been something special, something rare, something (as Monsieur Ribbins would have said) *je ne sais quoi* about her year, the inaugural year, that made it shine with a particular brilliance.

The handful of teachers in the Camilo Cienfuegos conference room collected their coil notebooks and ballpoint pens. Their sadness at being so unquestionably the nerds of the group tinged the room with a hue of blue, similar to the shade of the single highlight in the bangs of Orianna Nast. Rebecca surveyed the crowd: the denim vests, the polyester pants, the chunky necklaces, and large broaches. Substitutes, every one of them. Her hand on Lee's arm (the first time they touched). "Let's go, before anyone invites us for drinks."

They went to the beach. Each hotel had roped off a large section of sand that non-guests (at least, non-white ones) were forbidden to cross, leaving only a slice for the public in between. At the beach's other hotels—ones that were not all-inclusive—locals would gather on the far side of the rope, reaching over to sell liquor and snacks. But doing so was pointless at the ever-sated Atlantic Adventure.

Lee and Rebecca found a pair of lounge chairs beyond the floodlight of the beach volleyball court where a game was being played. A beach ball had been substituted for a volleyball and, from their far-off darkness, the two would occasionally hear a commotion of laughter and then a demand that one team "Take a sip" or, sometimes, "Everyone drink."

"What could be happening," Lee asked, "when *both* teams have to drink?"

"I've been thinking," said Rebecca, reclining into her chair while Lee sat upright on his in a lotus position because he wanted to casually impress her.

"About us?" he asked.

"There's an 'us'?"

"There would be," he said, "if we had an affair."

The volleyball game quieted, and the two of them listened to the sound of the surf. In the darkness, they could not see the ocean, but every once in awhile a bright bar of foam would rise and advance, hurriedly and out of breath, as if it had travelled from the other side of the globe to greet them, but got shy in the final seconds and burrowed into the sand.

"What have you been thinking?" Lee asked.

"You're not worried your wife will find out?"

"Not really," Lee said. "She'd probably think it a relief more than anything."

"A relief?"

"Last year, she asked if I wanted to have an open relationship, and I said I only wanted her, and she said my life should extend much farther."

"Further," Rebecca said.

"Much further."

"So what's the problem?"

"I don't see why it needs to extend—"

"No," Rebecca said. "What's the problem with having an affair?"

"Oh," said Lee, picking at his chair. "I guess I'm worried that if I do it, I'll regret it, and there's no going back."

"So we won't do it."

Lee stopped picking. "I'm also worried that if I *don't* do it, I'll regret it and there's no going back."

"So we will do it?"

"I don't know," said Lee. "It feels like one choice is definitely right and the other is definitely wrong, but I don't know which is which. What do you think?"

Rebecca sat up to watch another bar of foam advancing, closer than the others; but then the volleyball court declared "Everyone drink!" and the wave lost its nerve.

"Well, I'm not worried that my husband will find out because that is obviously never going to happen."

And through her certainty, Lee understood the larger implication. Her husband was obviously never going to find out not just because Lee lived in Kamloops and Rebecca in Vancouver (Burnaby, actually), but because there would be no future contact between them, no correspondence, no affinity built through this secret and shared experience. This would be an isolated instance, unattached from their larger, truer lives. Even if the two of them met at future TUP-CS, it was doubtful there would be the same spark, the same verve, because the itch would've been scratched and she would see him not as a person but a moment, one that had been indulged—like bungee jumping or dogsledding—and could now be relinquished. Lee was lonely in his marriage because his wife was not; and all of this with Rebecca threatened more of the same, because the affair had almost nothing to do with him. He was involved in only the most elemental of ways. Even the term "affair" seemed too resplendent, with its implications of indulgence, largesse, protracted pleasure. But what other term was there? A *liaison*? Too French. A *dalliance*? Too English. An *encounter*? Too extraterrestrial.

From the volleyball court: "If it happens again, we all have to get naked!"

"Worst-case scenario," Rebecca said to Lee, "I feel bad about it and have to swallow the secret."

"Let's take the night to think," said Lee.

Rebecca swung her legs over the side of the chair to stand. Lee placed his bare feet onto the sand and, in doing so, accidentally laid his toes on top of hers. For a moment, neither moved for fear that doing so would either scare the moment away or lure it forward.

What was Rebecca afraid of? That in doing such a thing, she would see the lengths she'd go just to sabotage her own life, to tear it down and build anew. The husband, the job, and then, too, there was her five-year-old son, whom she hadn't mentioned to Lee but only because she didn't mention him to anyone because doing so made her feel old. She had a good life, but that did not make anything easier; in fact, it did the opposite.

The waves broke the sand. She moved her feet.

The next morning, she joined him at breakfast. "Have you ordered?" she asked. She wore a floral dress—crêpe georgette and cut to the calf. Amongst the cafeteria of teachers (most of whose fashion sense could be defined as "comfy" at best and "Canadian Tire" at worst), the fabric's colour gathered the light like the lobby's mural, and just by standing in its presence, you were reminded of all the contortions a body could perform. Rebecca's husband had asked about the dress as he watched her pack, brushing his teeth. She said she was bringing it because there was a Gaudreau alumni dinner, but it was actually because the phrase "Havana nights" was impossible to say without images of pinstripe shirts, of hair held back with roses, of dancers burning alive on the hardwood. She lied to her husband not because any infidelity was premeditated but because it was such a juvenile and wanton daydream, she found it humiliating.

"Not yet," Lee said to her. "I can't get anyone's attention."

Rebecca spotted a waiter who was carrying one pineapple with two hands, and she left to intercept him. Lee saw that the dress, despite having a high neck, had a low back.

Rebecca chatted with the waiter, and Lee watched her run her fingers through her hair, the tresses falling against her shoulder blades. The waiter said something, she laughed, and Lee felt jealous and then ridiculous.

When she returned to the table, he was scrolling through his phone.

"Look at this," he said passing it to her. "They called in the military."

Rebecca read about the monuments graffitied, the barricades of office furniture, the savage scenes of state-sanctioned violence.

"I'm surprised they needed to call them in," Lee said. "I assumed they'd, you know, have them on hand."

The same waiter returned with their meals, and Lee tipped him ten dollars Canadian. The waiter bowed to Lee and then, more deeply, to Rebecca, who looked up from her phone to see his hinge of gratitude. She blushed as the waiter departed to his pineapple.

Lee asked, "What did you two talk about?"

"Pardon?"

"You two. What did you talk about?"

"Oh, he doesn't speak English."

"What language were you speaking?"

"The language of food." She pointed at his meal and spoke with slow exaggeration. "Juevos. Rancheros." She pointed at her own. "Lox."

"That's all," Lee said, the sentence halfway between query and accusation.

Rebecca saw the time on Lee's phone, handed it back to him. "We should get going," she said, wrapping her bagel in a napkin. "First seminar's in five."

"But I haven't started yet."

"Take the plate with you," she said. "Eat it on the walk."

"You can do that?"

Rebecca shrugged. "Here, you can do anything you want."

Their conversation seemed, of its own accord, to always come back to Rebecca's unanswered question—in a wide and elliptical orbit, like the moon: the farther it faded, the more tidal its return.

When Lee arrived at the door of the Camilo Cienfuegos conference room, he didn't know what to do with the empty plate. He searched for a table or ledge, but finding none, he laid his plate and his fork on the tile floor. And as he did so, he thought, This is something I've never done before nor ever will again.

The average attendance of the conference's first day had been so subterraneously low it was in danger of being mined by HG Energy and Minerals. In response, Orianna Nast had sent an email, saying she was "confident to the point of insistent" that the second day's attendance (and the third's and the morning of the fourth's) would improve *dramatically*.

"We would do well to remember," Orianna Nast had written, "those who, mere kilometres from us, are fighting tooth and soul for the right to choose the direction of their own careers and lives, for them to DEVELOP in whatever way they wish. It would be unfortunate if our executive were forced to reconsider such international venues next summer in favour of, for example, White Rock."

The email had been sent at 2:13 am, but because of its principal's office severity everyone had read it within the hour, even Rebecca and Lee who were two of the exceedingly few not partaking in any frat-house exploit but were in bed, alone and wide awake.

The warning had been given and the warning had been heeded. Rebecca and Lee entered the Camilo Cienfuegos conference room to see every seat—all eight hundred of them—filled. But the crowd had a sway to it, as if they were on a cruise ship at high sea, gently rolling this way and that. It was whisper-quiet, save for the slurping of black coffee. In the air, a sickening sweetness lingered. The hangover was so tangible you could taste it.

"You want to skip this and have another breakfast?" Rebecca asked.

Lee consulted his pamphlet: Reading Power, Whiting [sic] Power. "It's a two-parter. If we hooky this one, how would we understand the next?"

At lunch, Rebecca needed to call home, and Lee was alone at the patio table of the resort's Chinese restaurant, Five Point Star.

At any gathering of educators, someone eating alone constitutes a Greek tragedy, and Lee was immediately joined by two men: Andrew (grade three homeroom) and Angus (grade twelve biology and legal studies); both of them taught in Kimberley. This year, the conference had succumbed to chicness and forewent name tags, but Andrew and Angus had made their own.

"You looked alone," Andrew said.

"You *were* alone," Angus corrected.

"So we thought we'd join," said Andrew. "Is the moo shu good?"

Truthfully, it tasted like everything else Lee had eaten at the Atlantic Adventure. Did the American embargo, he wondered, include seasoning?

"I've never had moo shu before," he said. "So it's hard to compare."

"Is it pork or beef?" Andrew asked.

"Pork."

"Then why," Andrew said, "does it moo?"

Lee politely laughed while Angus rolled his eyes so far back he glimpsed his frontal lobe.

"Do you two want to order?" Lee asked, but Andrew said they had martinis on the way.

"Dirty," he added, holding up five fingers. "This many olives."

Angus told Lee about their afternoon plans: snorkelling then learn-to-surf then coffee roasting.

"Noooo," Andrew corrected, drawing out the vowel in the time-honoured tradition of those who teach the lower grades. "Snorkelling, learn-to-surf, coffee roasting—but first is the seminar on teaching diversity"

"Right," Angus said as the martinis arrived. "We'll see if *that's* going to happen."

As Angus stirred his drink and described the sandbar where the boat drops them, Lee's mind wandered.

Why couldn't he be gay, he thought. They were so much more evolved with this type of thing. Once, he was at a Christmas party at his then-vice principal's house—this was four or five years ago—and was getting his and his girlfriend's coats from the spare bedroom. From the ensuite bathroom, he heard two men whispering, Sam and...was it Robert? or Ryley? You know, the computer science teacher who, it later turned out, didn't believe in western medicine and so died of prostate cancer after forgoing chemotherapy for a mushroom and wild basil tonic.

The two were laughing, coquettishly, as Lee—a coat in each hand—cocked his ear to hear Sam ask, "Are you ready?" And the frankness of this question broke Lee's heart; as if the two men were on the cusp of some great adventure, an odyssey to a different world.

For Lee, it wasn't as simple as unfulfillment. His girlfriend (who, a few years later, became his wife) often asked what he wanted, what he liked. But these questions depended on Lee himself being able to articulate them—a feat that seemed as antithetical to him as flying must have to the people of yester-year, or the acceptance of Western medicine would soon seem to Robert/Ryley.

Lee had never been asked this—if he was *ready*—and Rebecca's question now seemed the closest he'd ever come. A hand had been extended, one that quivered with the same ache as his, and by grasping it, he could know another language.

Because of the subjects Angus taught to his grade twelves, he had long lost the ability to distinguish alert eyes from vacant ones, so he hadn't an inkling that Lee had floated into the realm of other lives. But Andrew, because of the grade he taught, could not only tell the difference but could anticipate the change before the viewers themselves were aware, and he knew Lee was lost. But he didn't have the heart to break Angus's, so Andrew compensated for Lee's lack of interest with a doubling of his own.

"What type of fish do you think we'll see?" he asked, and Angus bristled at the interruption.

"Did you not read the brochure?"

"I forget."

"You forget the fish or if you read the brochure?"

"I'd love to see a whale."

"There will be none of those at the sandbar."

"What bar do the whales like?"

Rebecca's hand was on the back of Lee's neck, and he turned at the shoulder to face her. From this angle, she seemed statuesque—not in the sense of topless and amputated, but rather like Athena, poised and assured, her mouth a slight frown, annoyed with the triflings of mortals.

"Is something wrong?" Lee asked.

Her eyes flitted to Andrew and Angus. She took a moment, forced a smile. "What are you thinking?"

Because she did not say, "What do you *think*?" but instead replaced the definite with the continuous, Lee understood she was not asking about the phone call. She was asking about the affair.

"Was the call bad?" he asked.

Rebecca sharpened her eyes and her hand slipped from his nape. "We've known each other two days," she said. "Don't be a part of my life."

And with that, she left.

For awhile, the three men listened to the clinking of Angus's skewer of olives, slowly stirring his drink. Then, the sound stopped, and Angus reached out his hand, not touching Lee's but almost. "Do you want to come snorkelling with us?"

The sudden transition from cruelty to kindness shined Lee's eyes with water, and he blinked to dry them.

"I want to," he said, "but I can't. I'm on the diversity panel."

"But you're white," Andrew said. "And straight."

"You don't know if he's white!" Angus said.

"I definitely know he's straight."

"I'm not *on* the panel," Lee said, rising from his seat. "I'm just the chair."

The attendance for Raindrops Make an Ocean: Teaching Diversity had returned to dismal numbers—most teachers believing that, having already suffered in the Camilo Cienfuegos conference room once that day, they had done their time and were free to carouse in the far reaches of the resort.

On stage, Lee took his seat behind the table and quickly found Rebecca in the crowd of fifty, maybe seventy-five. She usually sat near the back but was now a few rows from the front. She smiled at him; he at her. But each smile had an aspect of grief to it, that what was—or at least what could be—was no longer.

Orianna Nast approached the podium to introduce Lee. She shielded her eyes from the stage lights and surveyed the paltry crowd. "It seems," she said, "that we are not offering the best of ourselves."

The teachers studied the carpet.

Orianna Nast implored each person in the audience to bring two people to the next panel. "During our break, go to the lobby or the pool or the dance floor, grab someone and say, 'Hey, I'm cool. Come with me!'"

Rebecca, in her capacity as guidance counsellor, was in charge of hiring a former sex worker to come in annually and scare the grade twelves straight (a phrase now discouraged due to its perceptions of heteronormativity). Orianna Nast's directive to the room reminded Rebecca of what, according to the sex worker, a charismatic pimp had said to her as a teenager one Tuesday in a shopping mall, thereby charming her into a decade of prostitution and manipulation.

Orianna Nast shuffled her notes. "And now," she said, "let me introduce our panel's chair, a grade seven math and choir teacher from Kamloops who won last year's Gaudreau."

The panel was supposed to consist of three participants, but only one had shown up: a petite, well-dressed man (the only person Lee had ever seen wearing a cravat outside of a daytime soap) named Yordani. Yordani was born in Cuba, taught at Britannia Secondary in Vancouver, and—this was not part of his bio—had agreed to speak at the conference just to get a free trip to visit his family in the nearby city of Artemisa.

However, the roads had been clogged with checkpoints. That afternoon, the Cuban government announced that any dual citizen who "participated in sympathy riots" would be considered a foreign agitator. Yordani had spent his morning collecting the complementary chocolates, packing and repacking his suitcase, and deciding which road to brave.

Each panellist was slotted to speak for fifteen minutes before the floor was opened to questions, but after Lee introduced Yordani and said he could speak for forty-five minutes if he wished, Yordani shook his head.

"In response to the ongoing strangulation of freedom," he said, "I will not speak at all." His voice was hushed and trebled, a humility accentuated by the opulence of the Camilo Cienfuegos conference room. "Rather, I suggest we sit in quiet for the full hour to reflect upon how we perpetuate oppression on others."

Lee turned to the audience in consultation, his eyebrows raised. Of course, everyone hated this idea but no one had the gall to say so, and the sixty minutes of silence commenced.

It was to be the only time at the conference that Rebecca, head down in prayer, learned something; and it was to be the only time at the conference that Lee, eyes closed, did not.

The Atlantic Adventure's original building (which housed the lobby, the Shade Grown Coffee Bar, and a handful of managerial offices) was built in 1954 as the Soviet embassy. But by 1987, the site proved too small for superpower influence, and the embassy was closed for the construction of the twenty-five storey, syringe-shaped building that still injects the landscape of suburban Havana.

The old embassy sat abandoned, guarded by a university-educated anesthesiologist. Shortly thereafter, Cuba entered its "Special Period," a decade-long economic crisis that created over 30,000 refugees. Flotillas of homemade rafts were pushed north in hopes of America; the us navy, however, captured all men, women, and children, imprisoning them in Guantanamo Bay.

The conditions of the incarcerated were appalling and expected. The Canadian Prime Minister joked that the refugees had "made it to the most American part of Cuba," and, sure, everyone was outraged at his audacity, but also—as the PM himself had no doubt wagered—secretly thankful that the nightly news now stopped showing pictures of children eating banana peels behind barbed wire or gunboats overtaking teenage boys on rafts made entirely of empty gasoline cans; and thus returned to the clips of the Leader of the Opposition demanding the prime minister's resignation and the prime minister responding with the latest job numbers, and the living rooms of the nation reclined into their sofas as one would after an exceedingly long day on the ski hill.

In 2001, the Special Period concluded, and the Cuban government decided to celebrate by transforming the former embassy into a sprawling state-of-the-art apartment complex, named *El Atlántico* in honour of what was to be its endless and glittering quality. Rooms were to be given (free of charge) to those who had lost the most during the years of hardship, whose lives had withered and needed luxury to return them to patriotism.

You know the story: Equipment broke. Shortages occurred. The half-finished rooms were boarded up, and the anesthesiologist was rehired. In 2018, a German conglomerate offered the Cuban government to complete the construction for a 49 percent stake in the building, transforming it into the Atlantic Adventure All-Inclusive Resort.

But there were relics of the building's former life. The lobby kept the rusted wall of mailboxes for the cosy feel it gave the guests. The Camilo Cienfuegos conference room, originally slated to be the apartment complex's gymnasium, still had the upturned light fixtures, meant to reduce glare during volleyball games when the setter's eyes turned to the sky. And most famously, the resort's senior staff whispered rumours about the lobby's mural and how there was another mural beneath it, one which told a very different story about a very different world. And then, perhaps, beneath that mural, another mural.

Rebecca had read all of this in her research before the trip, sitting at her computer with her son on her knee, eating cereal without milk. But no matter how storied the resort's past, it could not hold her attention like the National Headquarters for Communist Youngsters, a building so self-assured, swaggering with both power and youth, that it could only ever be what it already was. No matter how much changed, there was no changing it. It would be itself until implosion.

The sixty minutes concluded with the beeping of Yordani's watch. He rose, and without speech or gesture, exited stage left.

Rebecca approached Lee at the refreshment station. "I didn't know you won a Gaudreau," she said. "Why didn't you mention it?"

Lee stirred sweetener into his coffee. "It seemed silly to brag to the person who got the first one. There was something so special about your year."

And with that, what was off was on again.

Outside the Camilo Cienfuegos conference room, the teachers in the lobby had commandeered the bar and now served themselves. The staff looked on, overwhelmed to the point of detachment. Rebecca hooked her pinky around Lee's.

"Hey," she said. "I'm cool. Come with me."

She began walking to the elevators, but her pinky held her back. She turned to Lee. "We have a twenty-minute break," she said. "In twenty minutes, this could all be over."

Lee followed.

In the witching hours of the previous night, the Cuban government had orchestrated rolling blackouts in Havana, randomly plunging streets into darkness to allow the anti-riot unit to move in with the freedom anonymity allows. It was a darkness into which people entered and never exited. In anticipation of another night of unrest, these outages kept rolling throughout the day. And while the disruptions did not affect the distant Varadero resorts (the "touristy ones" as Orianna Nast had called them in the welcome pamphlet), the handful of hotels surrounding Havana, including the Atlantic Adventure, were forced to rely on generators.

Disturbance was thankfully minimal, with the exception that the resort's eight elevators had been cut to three. Waits were not long but each ride was crowded, cheek to cheek, shoulder to sunburnt shoulder, backwards baseball cap to novelty sombrero.

Rebecca and Lee took the stairs, two at a time, single file. Her room was on the eighth and top floor, a request she had made mere minutes after her application to attend the conference had been granted. Lee's room was on the second storey but in the resort's eastern wing, a fifteen- minute walk across the grounds.

On the first floor, the eighth had not seemed far, but with each passing flight, Lee felt his face redden. Lee had always considered himself fit (he could, after all, sit lotus), so he was surprised by the rasp in his breath. During each school year's staff orientation meeting, Lee listed his hobbies as basketball and badminton, but it had been years since he'd played either. He had enjoyed them deeply but somewhere during the entrenchment of adulthood, each sport came to hold these moments of sudden stillness—the basketball circling the rim, the arc of the birdie floating—and he would see himself from the distance of his desire, high above. And from such a height, how trifling and callow his life appeared, spending his evening in the gymnasium of the same school he spent his days, his facial features no longer in a process of maturation but degradation. By this age, shouldn't he have stepped into some exquisite grandness? Because if it wasn't here by now, it stood to reason it wasn't coming at all.

Eventually, the basketball chose its direction or the birdie gave in to gravity, and the feeling would be blurred by frenzy. But such bouts became more and more common until, with time, he stopped showing up, choosing to surrender these parts of himself rather than be alone with them.

In the stairwell, Rebecca and Lee climbed higher, the doors of other floors passing by, and Lee thought that behind each door was a different version of his life, but one he could know only by abandoning this one. Higher, higher still, as if they were ascending into the sun, and he felt his gaze become untethered and begin to float upwards—a lightheadedness—so he ratcheted his eyes back to earth: to the rise and fall of Rebecca's floral dress. Each time she took a step, the hem rode up, exposing the bend of her knee, the pulse of her tendons, the rise of her Achilles, and the flex of her ankle.

For the first time, Lee considered the physicality of the act. Which position, he wondered. Or rather, positions? And kissing: on the mouth? And there would also come that moment, of when everything was off but the socks. And how to get free of them without bending into that exposing squat, all balls and anus, a prospect almost as unattractive as simply leaving them on.

The door to the seventh floor passed, and so, too, a life; and Lee asked Rebecca, "What was your phone call about?"

"Phone call?"

"At lunch. You called home and—"

"We're having problems," Rebecca said. "Me and my husband. My husband and me."

"I'm sorry," said Lee.

"Me too," said Rebecca, but it wasn't true: she wasn't sorry. Though she wasn't sorry because it hadn't happened. In fact, the call had been lovely. Her husband didn't bother telling her about what was happening at home (she had, after all, been gone two days) but had asked her all about Cuba. He never read the news so was doe-eyed about global events and had no idea of the unrest. "Did you," he asked, "see your Community Centre for Communist Youngsters?"

"Headquarters," Rebecca corrected. "National Headquarters."

Then, her son had taken the phone and told her that he missed her so much his feet hurt.

"Your feet?" Rebecca asked.

Her son was adamant. His feet.

He handed the phone back to his father who said they had to get ready because they were going to the Harrises for dinner.

"Check his soccer cleats," Rebecca told her husband. "They're too small."

Wasn't her life what everyone wanted? Why did something suddenly stop being good enough the moment it happened?

In the stairwell, they turned the switchback, and the eighth-floor door came into view. She listened to Lee's huffing.

Surely, she thought, everyone must go through this. Wasn't it all the more likely she *did* want this life but could only understand its worth by risking it?

They were through the stairwell's door and then at her room's. Lee was breathless.

It's true, the heart wants what it wants; but what if the heart wants for nothing at all?

Rebecca felt her pockets, said she'd left her key downstairs.

The next panel was Dodging the Question: The Ethics of Dodgeball. The crowd was modest though certainly larger than the last. The seats were half full, or—if you were a Canadian History teacher—half empty, though the size of the audience had much less to do with gym class morality and much more to do with the sun-stroking temperature and the debt of the past fifty hours coming due. Everyone was hunched forward, buckled into themselves, sleeping off their sins.

They watched the seminar, and when it ended (with an emotional slideshow set to Bob Dylan's "Blowin' in the Wind"), the audience startled awake and zombie-walked out the door. But neither Rebecca nor Lee got up. Both of them had too much on their minds for dinner. Besides, if they left this room, they'd have to go to another. But which one? On the elevator ride down, they had left it unclear if they were going to grab the key or stay for the panel, and neither wanted to ask for clarification because the other would say, "I'm not sure. What do you want?" And so they remained in the Camilo Cienfuegos conference room, the only two in the eight hundred chairs. They had only tonight and tomorrow.

To save the generators' electricity, the resort switched off the lights and all that remained in the windowless room was the red glow of the fire exit sign. The staff—more shadow than human—moved in from the wings to clean the stage.

Rebecca and Lee watched them rearrange the table and podium for the evening's lectures: the first being Intelligent Design(s); the second, Dare 2 Dance: Physical Literacy. These staff, Rebecca knew, were the staff that guests were not supposed to see—those who were hidden from the limelight of the bar and buffet. They were old, palsied, and walked with various limps. One man in particular was hunchbacked, but when he picked up his mop to push it across the stage, his crook put him in such a perfect posture for the task that Rebecca wondered if it was coincidence or cause.

She watched him mop, back and forth, and she said, "How do you know the life you have is the one you're meant to be living?"

Lee assumed the question was for him and replied, "Isn't that like asking, how do I know these shoes are the ones I was meant to buy?"

In the darkness, Rebecca and Lee were close enough to see the other's face. To Lee, Rebecca shone like cartoon temptation, crimson and neon; to Rebecca, Lee seemed on the verge of fading, the last gasp of colour.

"Do you realize," Rebecca said, "that in the future, we are released from this decision because we have already made it?" (This, of course, was what she told students torn between which university to attend.)

"Sounds nice," said Lee.

"But how to get from here to there?"

They stayed for Intelligent Design(s), and they stayed for Dare 2 Dance. But it would prove the final time either would be in the Camilo Cienfuegos conference room. When the second lecture had finished, and Orianna Nast dismissed everyone—all thirty-six of them—Rebecca and Lee went out through the lobby, beneath the mural, past the pool, cabana bar, kayak stand, and to the beach.

To compensate for the lack of Havana nightlife, the resort had set up a platform and light show and hired a DJ (DJ Cuba Libre). In the blast of bass, the mob of teachers moved as one synthesized mass, and the rumble vibrated the tectonic plates, the very seams of the Earth.

Andrew and Angus emerged from the crowd, and Andrew whispered something to Lee but which Lee couldn't hear, and Angus handed Rebecca a bottle of rum. The two men disappeared back into the bodies, and Rebecca put her mouth against Lee's ear, hollering to be heard. "Do you want to go," she asked, pausing to drop the bottle in the sand, "to the water?"

The tide was out and they stepped into the ankle-deep sea. Lee rolled up his chinos; Rebecca's dress swished above the surf. They waded into the warmth, leaving the crowd behind.

Lee, from Kamloops, wasn't familiar with the ocean and its tides, and he kept thinking that eventually the bottom would have to drop. But Rebecca, from Vancouver (Burnaby, actually), knew they had a long way to go.

"We will go until our feet don't touch," she said, "and then we will tread, and we will make our decision before we return."

Lee nodded and took her hand to steady himself as the waves broke against his knees. They would make their decision; in the future, the decision had already been made. Sometimes, Lee thought, the only thing that separates us from strip-mall psychics is that they're not afraid to admit they know what's coming.

The crowd disappeared from sight and sound. The ocean floor descended: the water at their thighs, waist, stomach, soaking Lee's T-shirt while Rebecca's dress bloomed around. But then the sandbar arrived and they were standing on the surface, the very skin of the moment, and their clothes clung so tight nothing was hidden.

Behind them, the resort twinkled. Each pinprick of light was from a window, behind which was a room—and inside, a life being lived. And out to their right, westwards, the orange smudge of Havana aflame swelled in the night. The columns of smoke rose from the skyline to become a skyline all their own, of a larger, truer world. And somewhere in that glow was the National Headquarters for Communist Youngsters, where desks were being thrown out of windows and their students soon after them; and deep in the walls: a curl of smoke runs its finger beneath the seams.

Having waded between these two worlds, Rebecca and Lee's own choice suddenly appeared so minute, so inconsequential, that their decision did not matter. Truly, it was embarrassing they'd squandered so much time considering it.

And to Lee, this thought left a plunge in his stomach like having missed the final stair. His life was never to be sung about, never to be noted, because those things happened only to other people. He had believed that if he continued to strive, both in work and life, that in his small yet diligent way, he would one day become someone else. But then he remembered the small fold of bills—their paper-thin hope—that he had left on his chair in the Camilo Cienfuegos conference room, a little something for the overnight staff, and he knew he would never escape himself.

Though to Rebecca, this thought of irrelevance proved the opposite. Since her and Lee's decision—any decision, really—did not matter, she was free, fully, and she felt like the ocean, with neither border nor containment. Each ensuing moment, by its very nature, was new—pure potential; and while it might not be possible to start over, it is always possible to start again. Not only possible but persistent. Indeed, it was already happening. The thin waves that rolled across her ankles were dead set on the shoreline, where they would push and retreat and push again. Beneath the mural, there is another mural. And beneath that mural, another again. But there is also one more, on top of what's present, unseen but its paint already mixed and stored at the overseas factory.

At the slam poetry open mic, the emcee is onstage, waiting for quiet. You are aware you haven't put your name in the hat, yet as you watch his hand root through the folded slips, you are so sure—confident to the point of insistence—that he will call for you.

OUR OVERLAND OFFENSIVE TO THE SEA

The eight-acre boundary of Nations at War is marked by the bright yellow tape of a crime scene. Only our southern boundary is tapeless, marked instead by the Manitoban shores of Lake of the Woods, along which Brandon (Armed Robbery) and I venture at daybreak. We have been charged with scouting the Nationalists's advance. Out on the freshwater sea, the morning's first jet skis are already carving their figure-eights.

Colonel Jared has long lobbied to get those future machines barred from the bay, as they do nothing but mock our historicity. But his objections strike me as somewhat hypocritical, since it was only during his tenure as a powerboat mechanic that he realized touristing sportsmen did not know Canada never had a civil war, and so—after an RV vacation to Gettysburg—he decided to create one: The Rancher Rebellion led by cattleman extraordinaire Baron von Hork. Conscription was optional but by far our best choice. As the warden told each of us at intake, the days of lounging in some quaint little cell are long gone.

Brandon and I, dressed in overalls and straw hats, journey into the woods. Two newlyweds peer down at us from the treetop viewing area. I know they are newlyweds because even though it is early AM, each carries a deerskin of wine, a gift Colonel Jared offers to honeymooners. Steam from the lake strains through the spruce, but from the vantage of the treetops, the newlyweds can still spot the Nationalist brigade, encircling us in their battle whites.

Upon arrival, guests are given a coupon for 10 percent off a future visit, a temporary tattoo of our logo (pitchfork crossing a musket), and a telescopic pole with an orange flag to raise if they wish to be retrieved in one of our wood-panelled golf carts. But customers are also given a history: "You are a victim," the welcome pamphlet explains, "of von Hork's hellfire that has been cometing across the countryside, west from Kenora and now northwards to Hudson Bay." Each guest is a ghost, encouraged to use his or her sixteen hours as spirits in whatever fashion one sees fit. They can haunt us, spook us, berate us with the many ways they have been subject to injustice. We, being lowly mortals, cannot respond.

So even though the bridegroom claps for the oncoming ambush, Brandon and I are caught unawares when the Nationalists let loose their buckshot, and Brandon's chest sends forth spurts of gore. While the soldiers reload, I turn-tail into the trees, leaving Brandon begging for mercy, and the bridegroom suckles the wine sack, as the bride turns to her better half and says, "I never dreamed it would be this authentic."

I, too, have dreams. I am enlisted until my sixty-ninth birthday. I have yet to have a birthday party since my twenty-fourth (the night that landed me in all this trouble), but I will be celebrating my seventieth atop two of the boulder islands of the north Pacific, just enough room for a house on one and a cabin on the other, which I will operate as a bed and breakfast. And every dawn, I will kayak over the morning meal—a metal tray and dome battened to the bow—paddling to my guests' bedroom balcony to say, "Lookie-loo what the tide's washed in."

By midmorning you can tell it is going to be a sizzler. During an exchange of gunfire along the riverbed, a heavy-set ghost succumbed to the heat and fainted. Since he was from a southern state, his agricultural attire allowed the two stretcher bearers—Tom (Drunk and Disorderly, Assault on a Police Officer) and Clarence (Drugs)—to assume he was a fellow rancher, newly conscripted. They whispered their compliments on his acting and stretchered his limp body to the green room where he resurrected to Tom and Clarence buck naked, changing out of their battle garb, and reminiscing about West Edmonton Mall's waterslide park.

Do I need to say that Colonel Jared is unamused? We are to remain in character for every second, every waking moment. "Even when you believe yourself not being watched," Colonel Jared oft warns. And day after day, we have witnessed our former and current selves becoming inextricably entwined. I have heard actors playing Hamlet note the same phenomenon.

Colonel Jared has reimbursed the southern ghost's cost of admission and is presently counterfeiting a ream of internet reviews to compensate for our new two-star rating.

"Another word for 'stupendous'?" he shouts from his saloon office to Wally (Assault and Battery) who had previously been an English professor.

"Egregious," Wally says and then flattens his straw hat against his head, marching off to aid our counter-offensive along the riverbed. I am scripted to accompany him, but I spot a fox by the refuse barrels. He lets me follow him for a full six minutes before he scampers beyond the yellow tape.

The ghosts' luncheon is cut short by William (Drugs) sprinting into the mess hall, followed hotly by a Nationalist lieutenant in his battle whites. Like all Nationalists, the lieutenant is an apprentice from the acting school in Kenora and currently lodges at the nearby Motel 6. The motel's laundry service is unrivalled, and his uniform is so starched that you can hear the creases crack. He catches William by the suspenders and launches him onto the table, landing him atop some Jell-O salad.

The lieutenant takes William by the bib and demands he reveal the Baron's route to Hudson Bay.

"We are not trying to fight," William whimpers. "We are trying to flee."

But the lieutenant does not believe him. Indeed, his men have tortured the testimony out of those who swear the very opposite. The lieutenant, improvising slightly, begins cramming Jell-O into William's mouth. William chokes and spews but the lieutenant keeps cramming and cramming until his victim stills.

I have been peering through the slit the door hinge allows. I am supposed to enter and scare off the lieutenant and save dear William, though I have never mustered the courage. But nobody is much bothered. The lieutenant does not mind adding this level of stage combat to his curriculum vitae and William does not mind being rescripted to golf cart duty for the rest of the day.

Once the lieutenant leaves and the ghosts have filtered from the hall, I creep out of the closet to stand over William's cooling body, give him the all-clear, and let him gasp the life back into himself.

At 13:30, moments before the chiming of the snack-time triangle, we are trumpeted to Town Square. The flagpole flies the banner of von Hork: a winged horse backlit by blue sky. Johnathon (Break and Enter, Assault with a Deadly Weapon, Forced Confinement) is standing in the pole's shadow, his head hung.

Robert (Drugs) whispers to me that a group of tattletale seniors overheard Johnathon asking Ian (Identity Theft, Fraud) if he could loan him some money to buy his daughter a box of white chocolates for her birthday.

"During the Rancher Rebellion," Colonel Jared announces, "men were not speaking of white chocolate!"

Johnathon lifts his face. He is weeping.

"They were speaking," Colonel Jared says, "of freedom!"

A pitter-patter of arthritic applause.

Colonel Jared snaps his fingers, and George (Manslaughter) and Duncan (Drugs) sling their muskets over their shoulders and frog-march Johnathon to the gates. He will now return to the sanitation department, where the skinners work and the soap swells the hands into lobsters.

William arrives on the golf cart, fiddle music cranked on the stereo, and whisks the tattletale seniors to snack. And they, so smitten with the thought of sugar, have already let go their grievances.

Myself and five others are piling sandbags along Wild Hawk Hill. Reconnaissance has informed us that the Nationalists will storm this summit by evening.

Along the hillock, a man glides by with his wife and daughter pointing at the stream below. "And there—why do they not include this?—is where the heavy cavalry outflanked von Hork's western advance, pivoting him northwards."

A woman, wearing a von Hork visor from the gift shop, interrupts. "But a latrine digger told me von Hork's western advance was plagued by destiny."

"Dysentery," the man corrects. "And von Hork used the Indian medicine to cure his army."

One of the sandbaggers, Daryl (Drugs), is Anishinaabe. In fact, because of what I have come to understand as the systemic prejudice of our contemporary court system, most of my fellow ranchers are Indigenous and have their own grumblings about the fictitious nature already found in our history. Colonel Jared, however, says to keep the past in the past, so shut up and shine your musket.

I look to Daryl to confirm or deny the man's declaration, but Daryl has moseyed off with the man's wife, the two now tight in close-quarter conversation. She is tracing her fingertips along the barrel of Daryl's rifle. Colonel Jared used to get furious when Daryl chatted up the guests. "But they are ghosts," Daryl defended, "and my people commune with the dead." Colonel Jared said fine but he had to commune with the male dead as well, but Daryl said, "The soul knows no gender." Colonel Jared did not respond, only chewed his cheek, puzzled. He appeared to me then as a simple fellow, trying to make it in a world that had been unsimplified but by what he did not know.

The man is continuing his lecture to the visored lady. "During the Clash of the Creek, the pillaging von Hork was routed something fierce."

She inquires if the man is under our employ.

"No," he answers, resting a hand on his daughter's head. "But we are from Toronto."

Why do I not escape this life, follow my little fox to freedom? It has nothing to do with camaraderie or courage or the whipping we receive when anyone deserts, nor even for the Hail Mary hope of the federal reinstatement of parole. It is simply because of the question the yellow tape asks of us all: And where is it you will go?

Which hearth will warm my feet, and which cauldron will feed my stomach? Which beds will dog-ear their quilts for my oh-so-tired body?

And in those moments, it seems that destiny has delivered us unto the only place left.

When Michael (Arms Smuggling) exited an outhouse, a Nationalist scout was waiting and clubbed his musket into Michael's mouth.

"Where were you?" Michael demands of me in the medical cabin. "We were to patrol together."

"Have I told you about the fox?" I say.

But before I can describe the fur, the nose, the quaintness of the paws, Colonel Jared kicks open the door. "Why are you here?"

The medic, Bill (Second Degree), starts stitching the split of Michael's lower lip while I converse with the Colonel. Because local anaesthetics are yet to be invented (and it would be frowned upon to give him uncut cocaine), Michael's whelps are pitchy and childlike.

"…and, sir, with Michael's charge, he can't be within forty metres of a firearm, antique or otherwise."

Colonel Jared holds up his hand. "I meant why are *you* here?"

I look at Michael, my bunkmate: his face so mangled that it no longer seems real but some macabre mask. "To see if he's okay."

Bill begins threading a needle for the upper lip, and a ghost materializes in the cabin's window. Crying always attracts them.

Colonel Jared places his hand on my shoulder and turns me towards the door. "The Nationalists are gaining ground," he says. "And besides, a bit of bloodshed never hurt no one."

Evening settles, and a group of us ranchers cook a kettle of beans in the buffalo grass. There is a provincial fire ban, so we use a battery-operated fan with strands of orange ribbon atop. The ghosts are in the cafeteria, eating brisket, discussing von Hork, and pounding their fists into their palms.

Robert (Arson, Attempted Murder) dips his finger in the can-cold beans and asks our circle, "How shall we live our lives once we are free of this?"

Donald (Drugs) remarks he wishes to raise horses. Matthew (Kidnapping, Human Trafficking) declares a desire to paint landscapes. Gary (Drugs) says there is no life on the other side of this, and Robert says surely the Baron will triumph, but Gary scowls and spits into the fabric flames.

I leave for my graveyard shift, which starts at 20:25 in the small cemetery on the northern edge of the property. For reasons inexplicable, the ghosts always have the urge to kick over the wooden crosses, and we are to upright them.

Allan (Impaired Driving Causing Death) and I arrive to an adolescent ghost punting his way through the rows. The boy spots us, and his face acquires a poisonous anger. He tells us how we razed his homestead: the flames lashing from the windows, the column of smoke vortexing into sky, the wails of his sister trapped inside. "I cannot wait," he says, "to see you suffer."

Allan stares at him, silent, and the ghost grows anxious. He boots a final cross and scurries over the picket fence that lines three sides of the graveyard. The fourth side, the northernmost, is marked by the bright yellow tape.

I remind Allan we are not to look at the ghosts.

"I was looking through him," he replies.

While Allan straightens the felled crosses, I am ambushed by anguish. I cannot help it. I feel so sad.

The graves, the crosses, the surrounding fence: all of it reminding me that I had been given a gift—of touching jeans fresh out the dryer, of smelling a neighbour's barbecue, of listening to gravel pop beneath a truck's tires—but I squandered that gift and no one is giving it back. It is not that I am unsure of my future but am sure of it entirely, yet still made to march through.

I have felt this way before. Once, I grabbed Allan by the shoulders and shook him violent. "We aren't alive," I said, my voice rickety. "Aren't alive at all!"

Two ghosts were urinating on the graves and ceased, mid-stream. Allan held my face and said, "I told you not to indulge in Bram Stoker's *Dracula*." He glanced at the onlookers. "Which is the leading publication in this historical moment."

He then led me to the shady side of the sepulchre, lowering me to the ground and, as I trembled, put his lips to my ear. "Just look at the field," he said.

And I did.

Now, I sit against one of Allan's uprighted crosses and turn to the field once more. The neighbouring lot's alfalfa pulses marine green. The sun begins to set, smearing my shadow beyond the tape.

21:00, dusk. The Nationalists march on Wild Hawk Hill. We hear their rumblings on the slopes below, but we hold, hold, hold, then—seeing the white uniforms—we fire. The smoke from our muskets thickens the air, and all turns quiet. Quiet enough to hear the trees growing leaves. We unsheathe our knives as the ghosts close in, dragging the fog with them.

A wild terror quivers the air.

Slowly, a rancher appears, stumbling out the smoke and missing an arm. Following him, a solider takes form, brandishing a shovel. Its movement conducts us:

When he raises the shovel, we inhale.

When he holds it high, we bate our breath.

And when he swings it into the splintering skull of the one-armed rancher, the ground explodes as mortars shriek from above. Rampage roars, concussing our vision, men cartwheel through the air, our captain's whistle demands we charge. A bullet nicks my neck, thudding into the cheek of the medic behind me, as I trip over one man strangling another with a belt. The smog reeks of burning hair, and I collapse into the mud as the gunfire volleys. A sergeant holds his own lung and whinnies a shrivelling scream while an officer hollers orders before a bayonet punctures his chest. A boy ghost wets himself, and his mother raises her telescopic flag, and William's golf cart weaves through the mayhem to valkyrie them away. The bride I saw in the treetops kneels beside a rancher and soldier brawling in the dirt. "Avenge me!" she screams to the soldier, swatting him with her empty wine sack, "Avenge me!" And the solider brings his teeth to his enemy's throat.

But then, the Baron emerges.

He is saddled on a black mare with wings war-painted white on her flanks. Having spent all day sipping cola in Colonel Jared's air-conditioned RV, he is fresh-faced and glowing. Calf-skin gloves to the elbows, knee-high boots, tassels all over. As a member of the actors' union, he is permitted nine minutes of performance before having a 75 percent rate hike, so he gallops forthwith into cannon fire.

Even dying, he is beautiful enough to halt time.

Head propped against his horse—who is also dying—von Hork gasps: "I had a dream of freedom." He chokes on his own blood. "But did freedom dream of me?" And with that, he expires.

But I have never seen this. Have only heard secondhand from friends, at least the ones not face-down. Because moments before von Hork falls from the saddle, I give pursuit to a man— a child, really—down the hill, tackling him into the swamp. Since his body is young and does not yet know itself, I am able to flip him supine and stab him in the belly. The blade slips into its handle and springs out again. We touch eyelashes as I stab and stab and stab, not a soul around.

After my lonely walk to Town Square (each time more lonesome than the last), Colonel Jared lowers Baron von Hork's flag and raises an anachronistic maple leaf. The ghosts hoot and whoop in the moonlight. They slurp cocoa and nibble cornichons and warm themselves beneath the heat lamps, so happy with how history has played.

The Nationalists have been bused back to room service. We ranchers, who have been battling a sixteen-hour day, stand there dumb.

During my sentence, I have been married. Twice. Both times to the same woman. This is why I joined von Hork, so I could live in a place where I was no longer allowed to pin up her photograph on my cell wall. I do not blame her—not one bit. How could I fault her for refusing to let her life parallel mine?

The last ghost drives away, and Colonel Jared is golf-carted back to his RV, where, rumour has it, he invites the Baron for midnight sandwiches.

We trudge to our quarters by the shoreline. As we march along the flat rock, Carl (Drugs) reminisces about his bungalow that overlooks the Scarborough bluffs.

"You say something?" Carl asks, but I shake my head. While he informs us how the morning light tumbles down the slopes, I continue but quieter: "Lookie-loo what the tide's washed in, lookie-loo what the tide's washed in, lookie-loo..."

Darkness has emptied Lake of the Woods. The water is so large that it appears as another planet—one of perfect smoothness—pushing through our craggèd earth.

The ghosts of my past come to me in my dreams.

"Forgive me," I beg them.

"Tell us how," they beg back.

I startle awake and listen to the night crew reset our battlefield: the sandbags removed, the bloodstains scrubbed, and the flag of a flying horse is once again hoisted. It is the sound of the world being put back together. And in this half-space between alive and asleep, I am an unconquered man.

— *For Tim.*

THE GREAT
AND THE GONE

"Every magic trick," Harry tells me, "is the same."
My head is propped with pillows as I watch her lean against the doorframe in her flannel nightgown.

"You get something, you lose it, you get it back."

She is presenting my mouthguard in her palm. She closes her hand, rotates her wrist, and then, palm facing the ground, unfurls her fingers. Nothing. Reversing the action, she summons the mouthguard to return.

I say, "Let's see you do that naked."

Outside, the sirens of the city howl, their bright lights finding her face, losing it, finding it again.

The cake's seventeen candles tell you that the birthday girl has already decided how much wonder she'll let this world get away with. Harry lights the cheque on fire, the one she plucked from an envelope atop the tower of presents. The cheque disappears into ash and Harry flinches back her hand, dropping the smouldering paper into a bowl. She frowns. "That wasn't supposed to burn so fast," she says, turning the bowl upside down, and ash showers the carpet.

"Who's going to vacuum that?" Birthday Girl demands.

I glare with such ferocity you'd think I was the sorcerer.

Harry feigns deafness. "I'll need some help for this next trick."

Usually, the hardest part of my job is choosing a volunteer, all those hands fireworking into the air. But today, the crossed arms of the crowd are holding out for power.

Of course, we have a plan for this. I raise my own hand and Harry chooses me. It's a bit less dramatic—my producing the completely normal rope, my verifying the completely normal rope, my being gobsmacked when the completely normal rope disappears into Harry's mouth and is then wincingly pulled out of her nose—but judging by the class photo taped to the dart board, the last thing this crowd needs is more drama.

Birthday Girl shouts, "Look at her sleeves!"

"Look at your life," I reply.

Harry's hand on the small of my back. In her palm, I feel the corners of a tightly folded cheque.

The first time she lost something—her keys—I thought it hilarious. "Just go like this," I said, waving a wooden spoon over one of her true crime books, tapping the cover twice, and then lifting it to reveal the bare coffee table. She replaced the couch cushions, took the spoon from me, and rapped my knuckles. But the next morning, I woke with her keys beneath my hand.

We'd been together two years before I found out about Erica, her daughter. A real-life runaway.

"Why didn't you tell me?"

She shrugged and slipped a slice of tomato into her mouth. "I thought you wouldn't want to know."

Tonight, getting ready for bed, I ask again what we should do for her birthday. "Fifty-three," I say, washing my face. "Big year."

"Look," she says, "fifty-three might seem important when you're, like, what? Thirty-four?"

"Thirty-one," I reply. Yes, I know I'm thirty-four, but I also know she doesn't know I'm not thirty-one.

"Whatever. But when you're fifty-two, fifty-three is as nothing as you can get."

"But you've outlived Houdini."

Harry throws her head back and laughs. "Why would I give a sweet fuck about Houdini?"

From the faucet, she grabs a hair elastic and slides both her wrists through. She takes a dramatic inhale and collapses to the floor, her hands struggling for freedom. Her face turns red from holding her breath and mine does too from laughing. In an Eastern European accent, she gasps for help, but when my hand touches her wrists, the elastic's gone. Before I can stop myself, out slips, "Where is it?" and she replies, "Behind your ear," and pulls the bright blue band from the back of my head.

I hate it when she does that.

I like to tell people she seduced me off a street corner. I was walking home from Office Max, still in uniform, and stopped at the pier to watch her busk. Twirling a top hat on her finger, she asked for a volunteer. All around me, a hundred hands rose towards the sun. I was trying to guess who she'd pick and choked on my spit when I heard my own name. I stared, petrified at her power. "Ah," she said, pointing at my shirt. "The black magic of the name tag."

She put on her top hat and fanned a deck of cards face down. I drew the King of Hearts.

She said I looked like I'd had a long day and might forget which card was mine, so she gave me a pen to sign the back. Then—"just to be sure"—she asked me to write my astrological sign (Virgo), colour of my bedroom (turtle-shell green), favourite planet (Mercury), last book I read (*Into Thin Air*), years I'd been at my job (four), and least favourite planet (Neptune). But after each answer I wrote, she took back the pen, lost it, and then found it again in my breast pocket, belt loop, or beneath my collar.

The card wasn't the trick. The pens were the trick. Because by the time Harry produced my now magically mark-less heart from a shuffled pile, nobody noticed that she'd switched decks when I was pulling the final pen from behind my name tag.

In the morning, I yawn deeply and say I need all her info by the weekend. "That's when I'm doing our taxes."

We stand in the shower, sluggish with sleep.

I became Harry's assistant four years ago, but—aside from that clean-backed King of Hearts—I don't know how any of her tricks work. Of course, I have my suspicions: a Velcro ball, a fake shuffle, a rope that fits into a tiny pocket on the sleeve. But I believe our act is better if I'm bewildered along with the crowd.

What most people don't realize is you need to be stupid to solve a trick. Good tricks lure your gaze away from where it needs to be to where it's supposed to be, and the only way to figure one out is to be so slow that your eyes still dawdle on the spot they should've left ages ago.

"I always feel sorry for them," Harry said when I asked what it's like to be found out. "They think they've got the world figured, but they've only got the clarity that comes from being so far behind."

How did I know she'd switched that deck? Because as everyone watched me find the final pen, I was looking at her. And I'm still barbed with disappointment each time she returns from a Saturday on the pier, having stayed in costume for the entire bus ride home, and takes off her top hat to the dozens of pens that fall from her hair and cascade to the hardwood.

Each decade has its own style of magician. The eighties were the time of the red-cheeked comedian, most tricks ending with a daisy squirting you in the face. The nineties were the heyday of the Italian sex addict who plucked cards from the cleavage of stay-at-home moms. Y2K had the ice-eyed illusionist, scowling at the handheld camera as he floated from the sidewalk. Now, we exist in the age of the hapless nihilist, the guy who can never find your card but then, on the sixth try, reveals it isn't even in the deck but somehow got stuck to your forehead and it's all a grand metaphor for life, ain't it?

Today, at an after-school centre on the rich side of town, Harry has drawn her fourth incorrect card. "The seven of diamonds?" she asks, and the girl's face slackens with sadness. "The ten of spades? The three of spades?"

In a flare of exasperation, Harry throws the deck over her shoulder, and the cards explode off the bulletin board. And then, one by one, the cross-legged crowd gasps at seeing the Jack of Clubs stuck to the wall, the boyish smirk on his young face.

I found out from a photo. On Harry's mantel, there are grainy photographs of the greats. A couple of years ago, I spent an afternoon at the public library uncovering their names: the Astonishing Anton wrapped in his irons; Grendel of Germania and her wolfman lover; Blackstone Francis with his mouth pried open to show where he'd cut out his tongue rather than disclose to the King of Sweden how he'd turned barley into honey.

But there was another photograph: a teenager dressed in black and holding a single white feather. "Who *is* this?" I finally asked.

Harry finished slicing the tomato. "That's Erica," she said.

"Just 'Erica'? Not 'Estonian Erica' or 'The Exceptional Erica' or 'Erica the Bird'?"

"Just Erica."

"Who is she?"

And the room became so quiet it felt as if I'd been dunked head first into ice water. I stared into the pixels of those adolescent eyes: like any good trick, they hid the world in plain sight.

"Maybe we can go to that fancy butcher," I say as we brush our teeth. "Get you a birthday steak."

She spits. "Wasn't Houdini a vegetarian?"

The next day, in a university ballroom, we're opening for a Christian inspirational speaker named Wayson Cross.

"But is that *really* his name?" I ask before the show.

She says, "Don't linger behind."

I thought it'd be a good crowd, but everyone has such blind faith that they've no need to know how the apple was folded into the handkerchief and became a plume of glitter.

The bifocaled man retakes his seat. "Some things," you can hear him thinking, "we're not supposed to understand."

After our show, as I'm invoicing the manager, I see Harry watching from the wings. Wayson Cross preaches about how we are known better than we know, that we can't out-hide ourselves. "Do you understand what I'm telling you?" he keeps demanding, and his audience stands and raises their hands to heaven. "Do you understand what I'm telling you?" The manager asks me if we'd like to donate a percentage of our earnings to the cause of shepherding stray souls.

I am about to scoff, to laugh in his face, and inform him that the latter half of shepherding is slaughtering, when my attention is drawn back to Harry. Wayson Cross is saying that we either submit to faith or wander without direction, and Harry lifts one arm at first and then the other, hands still caked in glitter.

"Do you understand what I am telling you?"

At the bar, I let slip that it's her birthday. The crowd buys her round after round. Then, I let slur that she's a magician.

A man in a sparkly T-shirt demands a trick. "Make something disappear."

Harry swivels on her stool, stares into his eyes, and says, "You do not deserve to be loved."

He screws up his face and walks away. It takes me awhile but when I get the joke, I laugh so hard I can't see.

I always assumed it was drugs—maybe a boy. But after the bar, in bed and against my instinct, I decide I need to know. Through the lisp of my mouth guard: "Why did Erica run away?"

"I was once," Harry says, and her voice is a silk cloak dragged off a table, "somebody else." Her eyes glisten before she flicks off her bedside lamp. "She's the same age as you," says the darkness, "so don't think I don't know you're thirty-four." And suddenly my life has become milk-carton small.

I used to believe it was impossible to love someone you didn't fully know. But see enough pens hit the hardwood and you realize nobody loves the trick they understand. At some point, you've got to choose if you'll be slow and simple and figure it out from falling behind, or if you'll stay quick and agile and amazed at this world.

The sirens begin, swooping through our city, and I curl beneath the dark weight of the comforter.

For our second date, she drove me to the mudflats where a lone tent glowed. She brought fireworks to paint the sky. A shimmering explosion, and I turned to Harry and saw her face flicker like we were living in an old-timey movie, like we had figured a way into the distant past, where everything was either black or white, and the only sound became the crinkle of fire falling onto wet earth.

Do you understand what I am telling you?

THE UNITARIAN CHURCH'S ANNUAL YOUNG WRITER'S SHORT STORY COMPETITION

The dogs are in the field, circling the trough, their legs long and thin. Michelle walks out in her rubber boots with a cloth bag of pig bones slung over her shoulder. The bones rattle into the trough and the nine hounds gaze at Michelle, their heavy eyes drooping, waiting for her to nod. When she does, they set in. As the dogs gorge, Michelle glides her hand across their massive heads, the straps of muscles in their skulls flexing while they chew. And amongst the snapping of pig bones, she blesses them.

The deadline is next week, and I've left it until the last minute. The Unitarian Church's Annual Young Writer's Short Story

Competition, with a grand prize of fifteen hundred dollars. There are only three rules:

1. Stories must deal with issues of faith
2. No foul or off-putting language
3. Writers must be seventeen or under and enrolled full-time in high school.

Like the woman in my story, I'm having a tough time in my own life right now. My mom passed away two weeks ago, and I'm two months from my due date. Living alone in our house, not knowing how I'm going to make rent, I was expecting somebody to come and get me—a friend's parent or some government agency with the words "child" or "family" in it. Day after day, I have waited.

I wanted to write something I'm passionate about. At first, it was going to be grizzlies, but then I thought I was too close to them, and when you love something so much it's hard to talk about it. So instead, I'm writing about a dog breeder. Her name is Michelle, a Hebrew name which means "who is like God," but I'm not sure if that translates to a statement or a question.

Michelle breeds Great Danes crossed with some sort of Himalayan hound. They stand as tall as young horses and have sagging jowls; their paws are large and round as human skulls. But Michelle also breeds rumours. She lives a few kilometres outside the town's southern limits and nobody has ever seen her in the flesh.

Before she moved in, the house had been on the market for months. An all-female cult had been headquartered there. A grandmother of eight preached the coming doomsday and demanded her followers forsake all their worldly goods, sign over their land, and drain their bank accounts. Once everything of value had been given, the grandmother declared that it was mere hours before Armageddon. Making their suicide pact in the field, they were each given a handgun. After everyone had one, the grandmother pressed hers against her temple and said that she was going to count down from five, and all twenty-six of them had to pull the trigger. She said they had to trust her. Five, four, three, two. One. After the gunshot's echo had faded, twenty-five women were standing in the field, trying not to look at the grandmother's body crumpled and oozing in the grass. Eventually the women started milling around, packed up the clothing they still owned, and organized rides home.

Michelle moved in at night. The house is at the top of a long driveway so when people drive past, they're too far away to see if she's there and use that as an excuse for never stopping by. They only know she's alive because of the dogs. Once in awhile, they'll see them charging alongside the car, galloping on the other side of the chain-link fence, their great grey bodies, muscles rippling and mouths frothing, keeping pace alongside the car until Michelle's property ends and they collide into the chain-link. Each time the metal takes them by surprise. Some say that she's got a buyer, a tycoon in southwest Texas, who takes a couple hounds each year. Others say that she inherited a fortune from a father who ran an energy company in Louisiana. Nobody ventures a guess to how she got started with the dogs.

There's a story about how a black bear once came down from its winter den and wandered onto her property. Michelle's dogs set upon it with such madness that when it was over, all that remained was a deep red that seeped into the snow.

I used to be quite religious. Right up until a few months ago, actually. And you'd think that my fault of faith had something to do with my mom, the grand injustice of it all, but it doesn't. Shortly after she'd been discharged for the final time, she was lying in bed and called to me from the kitchen where I had been blending some carrots for her. She asked me to go down to the basement and get her scuba goggles. My mom had never been scuba diving. The only reason she had the goggles was because she bought them at a garage sale when she'd been told that it was a mask one of the divers used when they were searching for the Stimson girl.

I brought them up and, to my surprise, she asked me to put them on her. She was in a lot of pain then and she said that the goggle's pressure felt good against her face. So there she was, lying in bed and wearing her goggles, her carrots in the blender. Her body was barely visible beneath the comforter as she breathed through her mouth, her top lip puckered by the plastic. I stood in the doorframe as she breathed so heavily it sounded like the ocean—or at least, how I imagine the ocean to sound.

And it occurred to me that she must've known the goggle's pressure would feel good—meaning that, at one time or another, she'd tried them on. I pictured her waiting until I was at school, creeping into the basement to get them and then into the bathroom, locking the door. She would've stood before the mirror, holding them in place with one hand as she dragged the headband behind, careful not to catch her hair. I pictured her looking into her reflection and realizing that she'd never get the chance to wear them in the deep, to see that other world.

It was that image of her in the bathroom that swept the last bits of faith out of me. Not because it was sad or pathetic, but because it was so genuinely funny. After I stopped believing, everything got so much easier.

The Michelle in my story has a secret. Last week, a boy—a teenager, really—snuck onto her property. The moon was full and cast silver shadows across the brush. He lost track of which way he'd come. As he turned to look for the highway, he heard heavy breathing behind him. He spun around to see but only heard it fade into the distance. His heartbeat pulsed in his skull. He heard growling off to his side so he picked up a rock and hurled it towards the sound. In the spill of moonlight, he saw a shadow recoil. The shadow sunk low into the grass but then rose tall, swelling like a thundercloud.

In the morning, Michelle found his body in the centre of the field, mangled and shredded but uneaten, the bent grass forming a halo around him.

I want my story to be about guilt—who did wrong and who's to blame. I guess, if Michelle had just reported the death, it would've been the boy's fault. But she didn't. She buried the boy in the same grave as the dog who killed him. She didn't know for sure which dog it was but took her best guess.

Over the next few days, the police began looking for the boy. Michelle, along with everyone else in the postal code, got the flyer. On it, the word "MISSING" in large bold letters above a picture of the boy at his high school graduation. His hair gelled and parted, his tie in a knot so perfect it must've been a clip-on.

My mom had been sick for years. In and out of the hospital, in and out, and then out one last time. Nothing about it was a surprise. She died in her bed with her goggles on and the ambulance kept its sirens off when it came. The paramedics asked me if I had grandparents or anything and I said I did, because—technically—I do. At least I think I do. The paramedics must've assumed that they were coming to take care of me, but they're somewhere in Saskatchewan. I want to say Bethune but it might be Bethson. The paramedics didn't say anything about the goggles but just lifted Mother onto the stretcher, her body like one of those large, stringy birds.

As they were rolling her out the front door, one of them put his hand on my shoulder and said something stupid about how it will never get easier but one day it'll stop getting harder. He then pointed at my stomach and asked how close I was. I told him a couple months and he said that he was sorry that the baby would never get to meet its grandmother. But he said it like he actually was sorry, like he shared some blame.

When the three of them left, I didn't know what to do. I packed a small duffle with a few shirts and some socks and underwear. I wasn't sure where I was going, but I assumed I'd be able to return if needed.

Once I was done packing, I placed the duffle by the front door. Not sure how long I'd be waiting, I clicked on the TV, catching the last half of *Jeopardy*.

What is body building?

Correct.

I looked around at the empty house. The television shot shadows across the drywall.

What is a body snatcher?

Correct again.

The house isn't even ours. We rent it from the Helmkens. First place in the short story contest would buy me another month and a half rent. I closed my eyes.

What is habeas corpus?

No.

There was a pause while the timer ran out and the buzzer sounded. I felt the baby kick.

What is corpus delicti? The body of the crime.

The next morning, I woke up in the chair and felt the urgent need to vomit. Running to the washroom, I tripped over the duffle still waiting by the door like an obedient dog. Afterwards, I washed my face in the bathroom sink and went to the kitchen to work on my story.

I wanted to give Michelle some background, something to explain why she is the way she is. But it's hard to write deep enough to touch the root. Like, there's something you should know about Jay D'Angelo, the boy the dogs killed. But it's impossible to talk about Jay without talking about his mother, Margaret. And it's impossible to talk about Margaret without talking about her prescription drug problem. And it's impossible to talk about that without talking about the long nights her doctor spends alone, driving up and down the highway, listening to Radio-Canada and trying to learn French. Everything bleeds into everything else.

It's easier to just keep a static image of Michelle in mind: she is on her back porch, Sunday morning, watching her pack circle a frozen pond, their loose-limb trot. The night prior, a coyote was scampering across the ice and fell through. Even though the water is shallow, it was unable to pull itself out. The pond froze again, and now its hind legs are held solid beneath the ice as it scratches uselessly against the surface. Michelle watches the coyote snarl at the dogs in a bluff of violence. The dogs pick up speed and soon they are galloping around the pond, vines of drool dragging off their lips. A dog finally makes a move and they descend together. Michelle, on her back porch, listens to the crack of ice and bone, the coyote's whelps and whines, while she fingers the beads of her rosary and makes up the prayers to go with them.

I've tried to think of a set image of my mom, but everything I think of are moments I wasn't there for. Like the goggles in the bathroom. And I've tried to remember how she reacted when I told her I was pregnant, but I keep seeping back into when she told her parents that she was. She is alone in the kitchen, sitting at the table, and drinking grape soda from a glass bottle. In comes her mother, holding up her hands like she's a surgeon that's just washed them. But instead of being clean, they are gloved in blood. She'd just gutted the calf. Using her elbow, she turns on the tap and begins to scrub. Behind her, my grandfather enters, his hands just as bloody. As he waits behind his wife, my mom announces what she's done. "I'm pregnant."

Her mother stops washing and the three of them listen to the running water. Then, her father turns around and sits in the chair across from her and, his hands still flakey with blood, fishes out a cigarette, lights it with a match, and begins to smoke. His fingers cover the white paper in red prints.

"I assume," my mom, "you'll be telling me to leave."

Her father inhales sharply. "I guess," he says, letting the smoke stream out his nostrils, "you finally did it. You finally got out of here." Her mother begins to scrub her hands with such force that her skin rashes, and the cigarette smoulders until the room smells rancid with burning blood. Not that I know what blood smells like when it burns, but I imagine it reeks something between rust and vinegar.

Michelle peered through her blinds. Earlier that night, on the local radio, the announcer had said that Margaret, the boy's mother, had come forward claiming that the last thing her son had said to her was that he was going to steal one of Michelle's dogs. He was going to sell it so he could settle a debt that she owed her boyfriend.

Not long after the radio announcement, two RCMPs were at the front door. Behind the pair, their idling car spun blue and red, the high beams glaring into her eyes. Because her porch light had burnt out, Michelle couldn't see either of their faces; only their silhouettes. One of the officers shifted his weight and rested his hand on his holster. The other asked her if she knew anything about the disappearance of Jay D'Angelo.

She knew that once she said the lie, there was no going back. So she hedged her bets. "I've never met anyone by that name."

She saw something move in front of the headlights. She couldn't tell what it was, or even its shape, but saw something shift in the darkness. An officer asked her if they could look around her property but she refused. He asked if that was because she was hiding anything, to which she replied, "Plenty of things that have nothing to do with a dead boy."

"How do you know he's dead?" one of them asked, and without missing a beat she replied, "How do you know he's not?"

The cops said they'd be back in the morning with a warrant and the dogs should be chained up. "For their own safety."

She watched them get into their vehicle, sound the siren once, and drive off. Michelle then saw what had moved in front of the car. There was a group of ten or twelve people, and if she had been like her dogs, she could've smelled their thoughts. It wasn't hard.

On my fourth day alone, I started the cleaning. At first, I tidied up the mess I'd been making in the kitchen. When the people came to rescue me—whoever they were going to be—I didn't want them thinking I couldn't keep myself together. I swept, I mopped, and after that I started scrubbing: the stove top, the hood vent, the sink. I used a face cloth for inside the fridge, which was now almost empty. I took my mom's toothbrush, still in the mug by the sink, and used it to scour the grout between the tiles, and the minty smell of her toothpaste swelled in the room. I couldn't use any chemical cleaners because of the baby.

Once the kitchen was done, I moved into the living room. I wiped the baseboards, shelves, and television screen. I filled a bucket of soapy water and started shampooing the carpets. I can't remember my mom ever cleaning.

When I moved into her bedroom and pulled the mattress out from behind the wall, I found a clasped edition of the King James Bible. There wasn't any dust on its cover. It would've been nice to think she was secretly poring over its pages, whispering psalms while I slept upright in the chair beside her, pleading *Keep her well, Lord. Keep her well.* But I'm sure it's dustless only because it got wedged between the headboard and the wall and has been squeezed there for years.

There was a knock at the front door. I ran out of the bedroom, pausing to wipe the hair from my face and tie it into a bun. They had arrived; they were finally here. I opened the door, duffle in hand.

Mormons.

Michelle peered through her bedroom blinds at the people outside her house when another car pulled into her gravel driveway. The group was now twenty or thirty. A minivan parked and another five got out. She wondered how many people down there had known Jay. Not just known his name and where he lived, but really knew him.

Michelle's thoughts floated from her bedroom window, around the house, out into the tall grass, and down into the hidden grave that held the boy and the dog. On the day of the burial, the earth had been dry and the spade rang off the dirt. And so the grave had made them tight as twins, both curled forward with their limbs folded in. As Michelle's mind moved over the boy's body and towards his face, his eyes began to shine like coins. And in them, Michelle saw his childhood, flat and full of unknowable distance. She saw him being scared of thunder but not lightning, saw him sneaking bread crusts into the bird feeder. She saw him tunnelling into a snowbank and then watching his breath dissolve the flakes as he pretended that this was all there was in our white world. She saw him standing alone in a field scorched with sunlight, watching the cotton rise into air. And then, years later, Michelle saw his mother asking the priest through the confessional's slotted reeds how is somebody ever supposed to know what kind of human a person is going to be, while outside her son throws gravel at the endless stream of passing semis. And she looked into the dog's eyes, its skull huddled closely to his. In them, Michelle saw that when it had mauled through the boy's body, it was looking for something it had smelled inside him, something bitter and strong. But when Jay's insides had been ribboned onto the grass, it turned out to have only been anger—solid and slippery as a heart.

Another car arrived, and the sound of its horn whiplashed Michelle's thoughts into the present. She knew that she, like the crowd below her, didn't know anything about Jay—was just making these things up. But she believed in them with such conviction that the lie turned itself true.

She took a deep breath and opened her window a sliver. She smelled the exhaust from the idling cars, but the crowd hovered on the far side of the headlights so she couldn't see their faces. Hidden behind the blinds, she yelled for everyone to leave, said she'd sic the dogs on them. The crowd quieted. But then from it came a bottle that shattered against her front door, louder because it was night.

I'd missed three days of school. When I arrived on Tuesday, it was as if I had this force field around me, like when you chase one magnet across a table with another. But then, at lunch, Millicent came up to me and said she'd heard about my mom and was sorry. It was shocking. Not that she was sorry but that she knew about it. Everyone did but didn't do anything.

I couldn't blame them. I didn't know what to do either.

The day droned on, students offering their sympathies in the hallways or in notes passed in class. At the end of social studies, the last period, Ms Haxton asked to speak with me. She said she'd heard about my loss and was deeply sorry. She said that she too had lost her mother—"stepmother," she corrected—and if I ever needed anything I knew what to do.

"Do you have grandparents?" she asked.

I had learned from my mistake with the paramedics. "No," I said.

"That's good," she said. "Nobody should ever have to bury their child."

I agreed with her and let both my hands wander over my belly. Usually, I avoid touching my stomach in front of others—but this time, I didn't care. I felt the round warmth spread beneath my hands, and then excused myself to the bathroom.

When the villagers hear the bottle shatter, they know they've set the future in motion. Michelle runs from the house to the back barn where she keeps the dogs at night and slides open the door. All of them stare at her for a moment, their eyes glowing beneath the barn's lone lightbulb. When they hear the villagers running and shouting, firing their rifles, the dogs charge past Michelle, abandoning her.

She follows them through the moonlit field, towards the woods that grow on the north end of her property. As she runs through the tall grass, the rifle fire comes from all around her, her dogs whelping and whimpering. She sprints into the woods but someone is gaining on her. She makes it to the trees but then tumbles down a rock face.

Lying there, she hears breathing, her heart beating wildly. She picks herself up, ready to face what has been chasing her. And in the moonlight that needles through the canopy, she sees a shadow skulking towards her.

At first, I'd begun working on my story to keep my mind off my mom. Near the end of it, she was sleeping for twenty-three hours a day and it was nice to watch her breathe heavily and write about Michelle walking through a sunny field with her pack trotting beside her.

When my mom would wake, I'd read her what I had written and she'd nod along and then fall back asleep. She never felt like she had to share anything of herself when she was awake. "Make sure it has a nice ending," she once said.

I'm still writing for the same reason.

Today, I got home from school to find a letter in the mailbox that's addressed to "Current Occupant." The letter says that unless somebody claims the cadaver in the next five business days, the province will donate it to the university hospital. They use that word and everything: cadaver. Like they already know what she'll become, and why bother trying to change what's destined?

I pick up my duffle bag, bring it into my mom's room, and toss it on the bed. I've been thinking all day—calculating, really—and if I win this competition, the prize money and the money I have saved will take me to summer. I dump the duffle onto the bed. I go to the kitchen, grab a plastic bag from beneath the sink, and bring it back. I start pulling the drawers out of the dresser and dump them into the bag, but I stop when at the bottom of one drawer, I find a photo with the glossy side down.

She is young—as young as I am, so this must be only a year or so before me. She is at a Greyhound station, leaning against the bus's silver side, wearing sunglasses, a plaid shirt, and jeans with holes in the knees. Her head is shaved and she isn't wearing any shoes. There is a man beside her whose back is turned and his shoulders are hunched like he's lighting a cigarette. He's wearing a T-shirt, shorts, and steel-toed boots.

She isn't looking at the man but straight at the camera. And, at first, I thought the two don't know each other, but the way her hand is frozen is like she's reaching to grab his sleeve, wanting him to look before it's too late. In the window of the bus, right above the man's head, is a sign that reads "Bethlehem."

She looks proud and stoic. Content. But there's something about that contentment, like it's more surrender than ease, that she knows when push comes to shove, whatever she does, there's nothing she can't walk away from.

I feel the baby kick and a wave of puke churns inside me. I go lie down on the bed and take deep breaths. I focus on my breathing and I can feel the baby growing inside of me, can feel it swelling, pushing, realizing it's trapped.

I'd once heard on TV that after you die, they harvest everything. I think of my mom on the stainless-steel table at the university hospital. At her feet, a scalpel has unzipped the skin from her legs, the line running up her shins. And from her chest, sawed and sprung open, latex gloves lift out the heavy parts of her. But on her face, her goggles are still on, their clear plastic freckled with blood.

There's nothing that haunts you as much as something you knew was coming. At night, sleeping in her old room, I hang my dreams on the ceiling fan and watch them dance their slow circles above me, and they are soft and plush and safely held out of reach. Life, I am realizing, isn't short at all. Life is the longest thing you will ever do.

It had spread amongst the town that the dogs were loose. But someone had said that all canines were afraid of fire. So they douse the dresses of their daughters and wrap them around the hockey sticks of their sons, and while the children watch from the living-room windows, all the parents exit their front doors. They see something on the far end of the road. What was first just a shadow will soon be illuminated in the torches' gasp of light.

It is Michelle, riding on the back of a Great Dog, both of them bloody and ragged. As Michelle and the dog stumble past each house, the neighbours will wave their torches, the flames whispering their secrets, and she will know that everything up until now has been easy.

GHOST TOWN

"But the Mormon man still believed rescue was assured. Even on the scaffold, he held out for hope—even after he heard the trap door's release, even after he saw the space in the crowd where his brother had stood."

"Did he become a ghost?" I whispered, already knowing the answer.

A cow parted the tall grass to nuzzle the ground near my thighs.

Drummond exposed his neck to the moonlight. "When the body dies in a state of wanting, the soul lingers until it is appeased."

The cow stopped grazing to blink at me. I considered petting her, but she read my mind and trudged back into the field. I stood to watch her leave and saw the trotting silhouette of a coyote crest a hill. Catching our scent, it halted, raised its muzzle to the wind, and yipped. All around us, unseen others joined in.

I looked down to Drummond, but the billowing grass had swallowed his body.

• • •

But before all that—before the long grass and the livestock, before the Mormons and the moonlight—I was in a Parks Canada operations trailer, sitting at a faux-wood table with ten other employees. All together, we comprised the entirety of the national park's summer staff.

We crowded around the table, self-conscious and uncomfortable, as a lawyer passed around legal forms (which, as we were repeatedly reminded, were not affidavits but merely "fact-finding statements" and therefore any desire to have our own legal counsel present was woefully misplaced). The room became suffused with the tension of a final exam, everyone scribbling away, heads down, arms draped across their paper to cover their answers.

I wrote my name, Bradly Rainville, and read and reread the form's sole question: "Has Warden Peter Healy ever acted unprofessionally towards you?"

Behind me, the lawyer grumbled about his drive back home— the potholes, the passing lanes, the *fucking* deer. I had met him before, actually, when Arthur Healy, Pinch's son, lost a thumb in the log splitter. Back then, he had been impressed by our first-aid skills; he was less impressed with us now. "This is what happens," he sighed, "when hippies get government jobs."

But none of us were hippies. We were thirty years too late. This was June 14, 1995: a day after my twenty-third birthday and two days after the intent for the second Quebec referendum had been announced. The federal government was having a tricky time then and wasn't particularly interested in a national park scandal detracting from the noble majesty that, as our brochure proclaimed, held our country together.

"Mr Rainville," the lawyer prompted. "Please transcribe your answer."

I picked up my pen and, with isolated strokes, wrote one word: No.

Of course, this was not true, and everyone in the room knew it. Peter, or "Pinch" as we called him, had indeed made advances at me, as he did at all the young men. But any "unprofessionalism" was so harmless, so utterly hopeless, that he seemed to be doing so not to bring anything to fruition, but the opposite—to keep himself in check, like he was letting off steam in small bursts, ensuring he never boiled over.

We had been warned of the perils of perjury, but as I retraced my two-letter answer, all I could picture was Pinch, who had been sequestered in the operations building's fax room where he was now, no doubt, staring at his oven-mitt hands. A man so large and lively completely shrunk by shame.

I looked across the table to see that Drummond Kelver had also finished, and I blushed at the accidental eye contact.

He had large deer-like irises, naturally highlighted brown hair, and cheekbones drawn by a protractor. He left the top three buttons of his uniform undone and none of us (certainly not Pinch) objected to the alteration of uniform. And he had these shoulders—truly marvellous—shoulders that made you want to cast him in a Passion play just to watch him lug around a cross half naked. Needless to say, I'd spent all of May falling in love with him.

I glanced at his paper and saw it was blank. The lawyer saw this too and told him he was contractually obligated to respond.

Drummond stared dramatically out the window, into the timberous heart of our boreal forest, and replied, "I take the fifth."

Drummond was (still is) the only person I knew who could say stuff like this, both solemn and self-effacing—taking the world gravely serious while dealing with it all from an ironic distance.

Conniption rippled the lawyer's brow. "This isn't a prosecution, this isn't a trial. This isn't America."

Drummond joined his hands behind his back to stretch his shoulders, and this goddamn beautiful shadow cast itself from his jawline onto his clavicle. The sun across his cheek; his hair parting from his face; eyelids gently closed in the shine; "I take the fifth."

A couple weeks later, a beaver dam was discovered in the northeastern corner of the park that threatened to gag the watershed and flood us back into the Old Testament, so Drummond and I were exiled to dismantle it.

The inquiry reported a "series of unfortunate misunderstandings," but Pinch was allowed to keep his job. That verdict, however, only further galvanized the staff against him, so he abdicated his duties and retreated to the fax room where he hid with his FM radio. Even Arthur—his own son—distanced himself from his father, opting to extend his sick leave by claiming he still had phantom pains. As such, the staff was in need of an enemy, and because I had denied everything and because Drummond had invoked his misplaced amendment rights, their ire found us.

I came to believe that clandestine meetings were being held where our colleagues—for hours of unpaid overtime—hatched elaborate plans on how to make our lives a living hell. But hell has a way of bringing people together.

Drummond swung his pickaxe into the dam's mud. "How're you holding up, Bradly?"

"They smeared honey in my bed."

The pickaxe sunk to its eye, and he struggled to unearth it. "You used to be jail bait. Now you're bear bait."

At lunch, we opened our coolers to find two dead squirrels, and we were forced to admit that our hearts weren't in it anymore.

"My mother," Drummond said, kicking a small hole with his boot, "works for Prince Albert. It's a half-hour drive south. She could get us jobs."

I was going to say no, that I'd just take the bus back to Battleford and head heartbreak off at the pass, but I realized he wasn't kicking a hole but a squirrel-sized grave. And how am I ever going to say no to that?

Drummond's mother did not work for the city. She ran it. Named (and I'm not making this up) Temperance, she was in her second term as mayor and had recently been featured in the Saskatoon *Star Phoenix*'s Sunday edition. At the time, northern Saskatchewan was almost entirely dependent on federal stimulus. In an op-ed, Temperance stated the Quebec referendum was going to siphon funding away from infrastructure projects—projects which kept Prince Albert's lights on—and towards (here was the good part) "turtle-necked dancers in Montcalm galleries."

Drummond's parents owned two homes. One was an old railroader's mansion near city hall; the second was a bungalow in a cattle field thirty-five kilometres south, near the town of St Louis. His parents had moved to PA after his mother's election, and the St Louis house (the one Drummond was born in) sat vacant.

We moved in, and I followed Drummond down the hallway, into a bedroom. "Here is where we'll sleep," he said, and my heart elevatored into my throat. I tossed my luggage onto the double bed and twirled around only to see a door in the wall that opened to another bedroom, a bedroom where he was now unpacking.

I was ecstatic to be living with Drummond, and by "ecstatic" I mean equal parts thrilled and terrified. He was so poised—impenetrably so—that the idea of him clipping his toenails or snoring or grabbing pickles straight out the jar seemed antithetical to his nature. And at that time in my life, I spent large swathes of each day in deep concern over what was unnatural—or, as Drummond would have said, *super*natural.

"This was at the turn of the last century." His voice walked that line between laughter and lecture, before pausing to bite two cigarettes out of the pack. He cupped his hand around the lighter's flame, and his face glowed orange. "There was a man who died of hunger while travelling between the Thirteen Castles of North Saskatchewan, helping prisoners escape."

"Thirteen Castles of North Saskatchewan?" I took one of the cigarettes from his mouth. "Saskatchewan doesn't have any castles!"

"Don't say things that aren't true," he said.

"Show me one."

Drummond stood, his cigarette dangling from his lips, and squinted across the cattle field. "Which way is east?" he said, visoring his eyes from a sun that had long since set.

The tours were to run Wednesday through Sunday until the end of August. Drummond and I were given flashlights but Donald Stahl, Prince Albert's tourism manager (who once referred to Drummond as "the crown prince of Prince"), told us to use them only if it was too windy for our lanterns to stay lit. "It's all about ambiance," he said. "I once went on one of these in London—Ontario, that is—and it was so spooky I almost died and became a ghost myself!"

We took an hour to get ready, Drummond and I in the home team dressing room, our naked backs to each other, buttoning and buckling our Dickensian costumes. I often asked for a hand, but after help was given, he always turned back around. At 9 pm, mere minutes after sundown, we exited the dressing room and walked into the rink's foyer to stand in front of the concession.

"Welcome," I exclaimed to the crowd: a family of three sharing chicken strips, a single senior, and two couples with a sad idea of a double date. "My name is Bradly, and this is my partner, Drummond." Drummond tipped his top hat. "We will be your guides for this evening's ghost tour. If there are any mobility issues, please let us know. The city of Prince Albert would like to thank Canada Tourism for their financial support."

After work, once the nights had thickened with heat, Drummond and I would retreat to the cattle field. We'd lie amidst the wandering cows, their dense bodies gliding past, spiderwebs of snot dangling from their mouths. In the distance, coyotes yipped and howled, back and forth.

"Try not to think of the pain," I told Drummond. He was seated on the toilet, backwards, his arms crossed atop the tank while a vein of water twisted down his back into the towel slung around his waist. I stood behind him, dabbing peroxide onto a face cloth. "Rehearse one of the scenes from Donald Stahl's binder."

Our script consisted of four "ghost" stories, all of which concerned underwhelming farm accidents.

Drummond scoffed. "Those aren't our real ghosts."

"How many are there?"

He seethed as I applied the cloth to the gouge on his shoulder blade. "Countless."

"You sure you don't want to go to the hospital?"

"It's 3 am on a Saturday, Bradly. Do you have any idea what the PA emergency room looks like at 3 am on a Saturday? Besides, we all saw you with Arthur Healey and his thumb."

As I eyed a nineteen-gauge sewing needle, he began: "People think this place is too dead for ghosts, but we were built of unmet desire." His back quivered as I slid the steel into his skin. "The settlement was named after Queen Victoria's husband in an attempt to coax a royal visit. The prince promised to stop by, but he rescheduled year after year until he got a bad case of Crohn's and shit himself to death."

I sewed a cross-stitch and pulled the cut closed.

"The railway was supposed to cut through, but the CPR chose a southern route, and our already-constructed train station was too expensive to tear down."

All Donald Stahl's script told us of history was that Prince Albert was the sole constituency to have been represented by three different prime ministers—that, and how to answer a tourist who asks why we're named after a penis piercing.

"The twentieth century didn't smile on us either. We were the capital of the District of Saskatchewan, but when the region was designated a province, Regina took the title. The new government promised to give Prince Albert the provincial university but they put that in Saskatoon."

I found it magnetic how much he knew—of himself, of where he was from. He could talk for hours and hours, but when he was done, there was never any sadness of conclusion because somehow you knew there was always more. With him, there was always more.

"To make it up to us, the Prince Albert National Park was established, but that only gave us more land we couldn't use."

I knotted the thread twice and cut it with nail clippers. The wound's top half wasn't clotting, so I puckered my mouth—the cut, like a set of lips itself—and blew. "I hope this isn't one of your mother's good towels," I said, glancing at the now-red hemming. "How'd you do this, again?"

"I told you. I was in the shower and fell against the soap shelf."

"You just slipped?"

"Yes," he said. "I was masturbating."

My lips hovered above the wound. "Really? You're going to admit that?"

He gave an exhale so dramatic it was like he was quoting Shakespeare. "I will never lie to you, Bradly."

For all of July, we marched our groups through the streets and lamented the farmer who got lost in the canola or the farmer who developed a deadly allergy to pollen or the farmer who tripped over the milk pail and conked his head. At first, it didn't matter that hardly anyone came on the tours—just like it didn't matter that the Quebec premier, the fish-lipped Mr Parizeau, consolidated power in the legislature and gave himself the strength for sovereignty. Independence was so far beyond possible that Ottawa didn't feel fear. There wasn't any fear in this city either, and the few people who did come on our tours left pretty quickly. We went the entire month without making it through the script.

We did have one reoccurring client who would drop off his overweight Rottweiler named Charlotte, and Drummond and I would walk her through our route. I got quite fond of Charlotte, actually, and even noticed she was trimming down, when Donald Stahl found out and said dogs weren't allowed.

"In case a customer is afraid," I told Charlotte's owner the next night.

"God forbid," he said, snatching back the leash, "that someone on this tour gets scared."

Without Charlotte, we frittered away our contractual hours playing blackjack behind the Zamboni. I once brought a Ouija board, but Drummond wasn't into it.

"The boxer, wanting his shot at the belt, stayed late into night."

I can still hear him saying this in front of the passport office he claimed was originally a gymnasium.

"He was hitting the bag so loudly, that he didn't hear his wife's heels behind him. And his back was so sore that he didn't feel the slip of her knife into his neck. Late at night—when someone's left a light on—he is seen boxing his shadow. He is the ghost who does not realize he is a ghost."

• • •

At the beginning of August, Canada Tourism's funding for the prairie provinces was diverted—just as Temperance had predicted. We were now to be paid *below* minimum wage. Donald

Stahl, however, said we could start collecting tips. That was when Drummond's ghosts emerged.

Along with the mayors of Swift Current and Moose Jaw, Temperance had a high-profile meeting with the federal minister of Arts and Culture, a moustachioed Acadian named Julien Charpentier. The next morning, the *Regina Leader-Post* ran a front-page photo of Temperance in the middle of the three men. In the current federalist fashion, each man had pinned a maple leaf to his lapel. Temperance, however, had planted a shaft of wheat in her blazer's breast pocket.

Charpentier stated the federal government regarded each province as one of its children, loving them equally but for different reasons. It was Temperance, however, who was awarded the article's closing quote:

"I've been in enough marriages to know that if you've got to buy him a car or a TV or a billboard in downtown Montreal just to get him to want you, you're only making the divorce more expensive."

Drummond told me his mother had been married four times before meeting his father: the first when she was eighteen, the second when she was twenty-one, the third and fourth in her early thirties, and then with his father when she was thirty-seven. "She once admitted to me," he said, "that up until her fourth failure, she believed that if someone loved you, they'd never leave." He flicked his cigarette into the dishwater. "She now knows that isn't the case."

During the August long weekend, a Quebecois trucker parked at PA's all-night diner. On his rear fender was a bumper sticker that read, "Anglo Go Home!" By the time the RCMP arrived, the man's hands were left zip-tied to his side mirror, his ribs and nose broken, eyelids swollen shut. The *Star Phoenix* said he was incoherent, but that might've been because he only spoke French.

From the long weekend on, Drummond ended our tour at the diner. "The dead have much in common," he said to the crowd. "All these ghosts—the veterinarian, the blacksmith, the boxer—are waiting for something to soothe their spirits. And one day, they may receive it."

He raised his lantern and the light sunk shadows beneath his eyes. "But there will be no justice for the chuckwagon driver. He died wanting what he can never receive. He will be a ghost until the world burns."

In the front row, a young woman gasped at our glamorous tragedy.

I placed my hand on Drummond's shoulder and stepped in front. "Ladies and gentlemen, our sponsor bar, The Fragrant Fox, has some friendlier spirits awaiting you." After the chuckles died, I plucked Drummond's top hat off his head. "If you feel so inclined, we are happy to accept gratuities on behalf of our local government."

As a flurry of hands descended into the top hat, I stared at the hulking bodies of the eighteen-wheelers, their hubcaps shining like crown jewels. If it's true your life will greet you moments before your death and flash nakedly before your eyes, then isn't it also true that in the meantime your life spends its days waiting, far ahead, kicking the tires and checking the time?

"Pardon me?"

"I said, do you have change?"

"Yes," I told the young woman, and looked into our top hat, brimming with treasure. "Help yourself."

...

On September 6, the final version of the Sovereignty Bill was unveiled with flair at the Grand Théâtre de Québec. But the flair soon fizzled when the first polls were released and showed sovereignty to be trailing badly, each day nearing a double-digit deficit. Even Fate, it seemed, was a federalist.

By then, our tours had become so popular the city extended our run until Halloween. We were in the kitchen (of what I'd been nonchalantly referring to as "our house") when Donald Stahl phoned to give us the news. I was seated with my back against the sink, leaning my neck beneath the faucet. Drummond clicked off the speaker phone and finished rinsing the shampoo from my scalp.

"Bradly, have I told you about the drunk taxidermist?"

"No. Did he stuff himself by accident?"

Drummond squatted to my level and ran a comb through my hair. He narrowed his gaze and eye-balled what he'd take.

"He specialized in hummingbirds. When you walked into his showroom, you stood beneath a flock of green and blue like it was the northern lights. Out of his collection, the most valuable—the most beloved—were four ruby-throated males."

The scissors squeaked their little song, and my hair dropped onto the towel that draped my shoulders.

"But he liked rum as well, and soon owed the wrong people a lot of money."

As he clipped my sideburns, the story fell away. I'd thought he'd forgotten so I prompted.

"Yes," he replied, trimming my bangs, "I'm just deciding."

He continued: "Not wanting the cronies to take his ruby-throated birds, but knowing they'd find whatever he hid, he made an incision in his belly and slid each bird in. But he only fit three. For the fourth, he opened his upper thigh."

His hands brushed the hair off my collarbone. "The man bled out quickly. They buried him with the three still in his stomach."

Drummond's ghosts were without end. And hearing him tell these stories, I imagined the spirits lined upon behind him, like ragged and cheek-boned refugees—and he, their border into another world.

"Drummond," I said, "I want to ask you something."

"There's no point in asking," he replied, whirling the towel off my chest. "Nobody knows what happened to the fourth."

The morning of September 7, the referendum question was announced. On October 30, Quebecers would be asked:

Do you agree that Quebec should become sovereign after having made a formal offer to Canada for a new economic and political partnership within the scope of the bill respecting the future of Quebec and of the agreement signed on June 12, 1995?

Prime Minister Jean Chrétien stated that the question was actually quite simple. Yes: you wanted Quebec to separate. No: you wanted to stay.

"Do you want me to stay?" I was standing in the doorway that linked our rooms, and I'd closed my eyes to ask the question.

"Do you want to?"

In my self-imposed darkness, I stood there and didn't know what to say. My fingertips pushed my eyelids until I saw nebulas.

Drummond's stories grew so elaborate that they became these many-tentacled tales, and I would watch our audience grow tangled in his words.

"While it might not look like it now, this was a trapper's cabin. The metal teeth of bear traps covering each wall."

Everyone drew towards him, guided by lantern light, entering into a moment that adrenaline had sharpened.

"And because he was out here alone, he had no qualms with breaking the Trapper's Code, shooting cubs in the den and leaving the meat for the crows."

The eyes in the audience flickered with hunger, and I became slack-jawed with the idea that they were the ghosts, wandering behind Drummond and waiting to hear him shape their story.

"SNAP! He looked down to his foot to see he had stepped into his own trap. He didn't have the strength to pry open the jaw's rusted hinge nor the reach to the rafters where the chain was anchored."

What was my greatest fear? That I had already died, the life cleaved from me, and I was trying to figure which way my soul had split.

. . .

October was the month we split at the seams. On the seventh, Lucien Bouchard was appointed the Chief Negotiator for the "Yes" side—the separation side—and the pendulum of popularity swung in his favour. In his first press conference, Bouchard asked his province what was their desire, and it appeared that he himself was their answer. In response, the "No" campaign quoted auto manufacturing statistics, and Quebecers clinked through the night with the sound of a million minds being changed.

"Now, like this," I told the elderly man, rotating my wrist counterclockwise. "Good."

I wrapped my costume's scarf around his bird-bone wrist and splinted it with an anachronistic BBQ lighter. "It's only a sprain," I told him. "But you'll have a bad bruise."

He then leaned towards me and touched his forehead to mine. The grocery store's neon burned his wet eyes.

Drummond didn't miss a step: "So when we think of pooling blood, we should think of the blind grocer because nothing bruises like the human heart."

"A contusion," whispered the elderly man.

That night, after the tour and on our way to the cattle field, Drummond and I stopped behind the laundromat for a cigarette. Tucked against the wall, I held the spare BBQ lighter between us and our cigarettes touched through the flame.

There are always fictions you believe when you adore a person. I don't mean when you love or desire or trust a person; I mean absolute adoration: when you glimpse some pitifulness inside someone that they themselves aren't aware they're showing, and—for reasons you can never entirely admit—you choose not to exploit or ignore it but rather make a silent vow of protection. In the cattle field, Drummond lying beside me, I would think back to that dumpy bar lit with Christmas lights in Waskesiu (a town on the eastern border of the national park), when I was standing ahead of Pinch in the lineup to get a drink and found myself considering—seriously considering—turning around and telling him that I was not who I was pretending to be, and the only reason I stayed facing forward was because I wasn't sure he'd believe me (I wasn't sure I believed myself), and he would think I was pulling some joke or—worse yet—mocking him. "Two beers," I told the bartender, and I took the bottles and turned to Pinch, who was

watching the dance floor, and handed him one, and Pinch—
who I then remembered only drank gin—accepted the bottle
with both hands, smiled, and said, "I can learn to love this,"
and I believed him.

On the fifteenth, Drummond and I arrived home to the phone
ringing. It was Temperance.

That afternoon, Corrections Canada announced it would
be demoting Prince Albert Penitentiary from a Special Handling
Unit to a plain ol' maximum security. There were only two
SHUs in the country; now, there would be only one, located in
Sainte-Anne-des-Plaines. All day, Temperance had been in
interviews, punning wildly off the phrase "if the SHU fits."

"Turn on the TV," Drummond told me, then, back into the
phone: "What channel?" He shouldered the receiver and held
up eight fingers.

Jacques Chirac, the French president, was on *Larry King*.

"You didn't answer the question," Larry pressed. "The caller's
question was if Quebec decides to separate, will you recognize
that new government?"

Chirac paused. "If the referendum is positive," he replied,
"the French government will recognize that factuality."

"Fuck me," Drummond whispered, letting the phone slip
from his shoulder. "How many people with the initials JC are
going to ruin this world?"

"You mean Jesus Christ?"

"I meant Julius Caesar, but Christ works too."

"Jacques Cartier," I said, and Drummond added James
Cook.

"Jean Chrétien. Jacques Charest."

Suddenly, the list seemed endless.

PA had a park on the south side of the river, beside the museum. Past midnight, there was an understanding. The night of the seventh, while Drummond was out with high school friends, I went there. I saw Donald Stahl, Arthur Healy, and a few fathers from the tour. They floated between the trees, coming together in the dark. It's not just wanting what you can't have—it's wanting what you don't want to want.

Years later, I found out there was a real ghost of northern Saskatchewan—at least as real as any ghost gets. I was writing a letter to a man I'd met on a two-week tour of the castles of Scotland, and I was telling him about the Thirteen Castles of North Saskatchewan: a code name for the residential schools that blighted the region, so when the Mounties intercepted letters that described prisoners worming free from dungeons, they thought it all fairy tale.

During that Scotland trip, the tour guide asked me where I lived in Canada. By then, I had moved to a much larger city, but when I told people this, they seemed disappointed, like I was sullying their daydreams of snow-shoed lumberjacks living in a hinterland. So I told the tour guide what I'd been telling everyone: Prince Albert, Saskatchewan. I expected him to say he'd never heard of it, but it turned out he knew more than I did:

There is a stretch of railbed north of St Louis, along which a green light appears with nocturnal regularity. The light comes from a train that decapitated a deaf conductor who was inspecting the tracks and didn't hear the guillotine rolling up behind him. Even though the railway's been abandoned and the tracks pulled up, the light continues to glow.

The spur line never reached Prince Albert, and so the phantom light never does either. Drummond must have known, but he never told me. All those nights roaming through pretend

Prince Albert, while a genuine ghost lived just a little bit out of reach.

As I dropped my letter into the mailbox, kissing the envelope for luck, I walked home and admitted to myself that I had not only seen the phantom light but understood it. One night, in the cattle field, after Drummond had gone to bed, I stood in the tall grass and a warm wind sighed through the stalks. In the distance, I saw a small green shine. And I stood there for lifetimes because I was so certain—would've bet my soul on it—that my train was coming in, that the future had finally arrived.

"In the Victorian era," I replied to the teenager with a Blue Bombers jersey, "tight pants were fashionable. To prevent an unsightly bulge, a man would have a 'dressing ring' bolted through the shaft of his penis to be held by a hook inside his pants, discretely tucking his genitals against the leg. Queen Victoria's husband, our city's namesake, had such a ring. We are not named for that piercing but in spite of it."

Drummond asked the teenager if he could continue with his tale. The teenager sulked back to his friends.

"So late one night," Drummond said, "on the walk home from the park, Mr Toole ran into four students from his class. Boys he had taught fractions to, had taught French to. The boys spoke as one. 'We know who you are,' they said. 'I would hope so,' their teacher replied, walking faster. 'No,' they said, 'we know *what* you are.'"

Mid-October, and Drummond was still adding to the tour, perfecting our script. The audience gathered, leaning in, like he held the world's last bit of oxygen in his mouth.

"'Poltergeist,'" he said. "From the German *geist*—'ghost'— and *poltern*—'to rant, to disturb, to insist on being seen.' On autumn nights, you can still hear Mr Toole's phone ringing, hoping that someone will pay attention."

The teenager in the Blue Bombers jersey shot his hand into the air again. "They didn't have cell phones in the olden days."

My stomach seized. We'd been found out.

"Olden days?" Drummond said. "This happened last year."

One morning at breakfast, he asked what I wanted from this life. I considered the question:

1) To bicycle across the prairies.
2) A daughter.
3) To snap off my latex gloves at the end of an ER night shift and have someone already stepping on the garbage bin's pedal, waiting for me.

Of course, I didn't say any of this. All I said was, "To have three cigarettes in a row that taste like the first."

What did he want? "I wanna sit at a wobbly table in the corner of an Italian restaurant and hold up a thin glass and whisper, 'To us.'"

"Who is *us*?" I asked.

"Depends," he said. "Who are *you*?"

Irony unravelling into sincerity.

By late October, the nights had become chilled with dew, and mist settled across the cattle field. A calf had recently been mauled, so dozens of scarecrows were erected to keep the coyotes away. In the half light, the straw silhouettes were entombed by fog.

Earlier that week, a hydroelectric weir to be built downstream of PA had its federal funding reassigned to a town in northern Quebec that was named for the patron saint of criminals. I wasn't aware of the saint's sordid past until Temperance made tremendous hay out of it in the *Star Phoenix*.

But the next morning, the *Leader-Post*'s cover story declared Temperance had been having a year-long affair with Julien Charpentier, the moustachioed minister of Arts and Culture. Both of them denied everything, said it was a smear campaign by the separatists, but Julien had an incriminating history of flying first-class to Prince Albert every other week. The only thing he loved more than Temperance was claiming receipts.

As Drummond and I made our way past the scarecrows, I saw that they, too, had been hunted. Some were bent at the waist, their clothes shredded and strewn. In the crisp autumn air, the earth smelled of the snow that had not yet fallen but was on its way.

"I used to be embarrassed by all her marriages," Drummond said. "I thought they showed a lack of awareness."

That night was to prove our last together. Unbeknownst to us, Drummond's father was already filing for divorce, and Temperance was coming to stay in the Saint Louis house.

"But now," Drummond said, "I think the opposite. To lose and lose but refuse defeat."

We walked until the grass was tall enough that when we lay down, we disappeared. I never asked him if the affair was true because I didn't want to break our bargain. If someone is to never lie to you, certain questions must be swallowed.

"Bradly, have I told you about the ghost with the immortal heart?"

"No." I rested my head on his stomach to stare at the smear of stars. "What's his story?"

"Her story," he said. "One night, she had the sudden urge for a horseback ride. She saddled her mare and trotted the town's border. The next night, she had the same urge. The next as well. The next and the next and the next."

Every time he inhaled, his stomach raised my head and then descended it with the length of his sentence.

"This was a hundred years ago. Each night, she still circles the town, looking for what she wants."

"What does she want?"

"She doesn't know."

We lay in silence while I watched the clouds move in. "So how'd she die?"

"She didn't. She is the only ghost still alive."

The stars dimmed and with them, all direction was erased. "What about the horse?"

"What?"

"The mare," I said. "Wouldn't it have died by now?"

Drummond rested his palm on my forehead. "Maybe," he said. "Maybe she walks by herself now."

And I was in great pain then, when I rolled from his stomach and rose. A wind picked up, and a cold rain began to fall; and I was forced to concede that summer had long ended, that I had overstayed my welcome, that our train had left us abandoned. I turned to face what I guessed was east, to where our brittle country was breaking, and saw the storm had erased the horizon. The rain began to freeze, and I felt so alone because I felt like I would live forever.

Hope was, of course, on its way, as it always is. In a matter of hours, the James Bay Cree and the White House briefing room would say what we ourselves couldn't find the words to. And on the eve of Halloween, despite the sovereigntists having redoubled their lead, the blade would glide across our neck but never slip in, which was all the better because clarity only comes from catastrophe.

But in the cattle field, I knew none of this. All I knew were the grazing cows, who dealt with their hunger so simply, so indomitably, that they seemed the embodiment of truth: so shameless and slow they stood no chance against the teeth that prowled the perimeter.

Drummond rose as well; and he then did the kindest thing that anyone has ever done for me. Shirt clinging to his shoulders, he tilted back his head, exposed his throat to the rain, and howled, tricking the coyotes, one by one, to reveal where they hid and who they were.

SATELLITE

Sometimes, when we were lucky, the nuns joined us. There were enough skates to go around, and the good sticks were always set aside. Mother Superior Pamela used the CCM carbon fibre with the JetSpeed grip (offered by a family of six from northern Alberta), while Sister Jillian swore by a Hespeler Composite (offered by a widower who'd trudged all the way from Winnipeg, losing his wife and teenage son on the journey).

"There's no convent in Moose Jaw anymore?" Sister Jillian had asked him as she eyed the left-handed curve of the Hespeler's blade.

The man's fingers had been blackened by ash and frostbite, so he sandwiched the pen between both hands to scrawl his signature in the guest book, and he said everyone in Moose Jaw went topside a few years ago. Same with the convents in Kenora, Missoula, even the Twin Cities. "It's just you folks up here," he said, "and the one in that abandoned military bunker in Colorado."

"Thank heavens you made it," Sister Jillian said as she used a pen knife to scratch her name into the Hespeler's shaft.

"I'll be sure to," said the man, who—against his best efforts of mourning—succumbed to a smile as I escorted him to the Chamber.

On the rink, Sister Jillian snapped the puck to Sister Philomena as the play transitioned into the neutral zone. I fell back to centre where I intercepted a two-line pass from Sister Philomena to Sister Dolores, and I dumped the puck back along the boards. Sister Dolores gave chase, and as she rushed by—arms pumping—slashed me in the ankle. The pain went through the bone and I dropped to all fours, but I didn't call a penalty because if there was a ref, they never would've seen it. From the ice, I watch the waistband rosary of Sister Dolores snap behind her like a black tail.

If we had been living in a different time, the nuns could've gone pro. Out of us kids, O'Bryan was the oldest at sixteen, but the Sisters could shoot sharper and hit harder than even he. Our only hope was to outsmart them—difficult, since they saw the game from another level, one a million miles high.

Carl M and Sister Harriette were scrumming along the boards until Sister Philomena barrelled in and body-checked him off his feet. Sister Esther wheeled the puck behind her net as the nuns changed lines. Sister Martha pushed up her goalie mask, one that was the old-timey plastic kind because she said the full helmet with the cat-eyed cage scrunched up her habit. "Burning Man," she hollered, calling the play.

Sister Esther whirled leftside, and Matthias sprinted in to forecheck even though we were still changing on the fly, and Sister Esther deked him, spraying a rooster tail of ice, and pushed the puck to Sister Nicola who, without pause, chipped it off the boards to spring Sister Barbara who had Sister Francine with her as they charged towards me for a 2-on-1.

The rink had originally been built on the mountain's eastern plateau, but the winds kept carrying ash from the unseen cities below, and each morning the plateau was smothered with soot. Five years ago, we moved the rink to the frozen marsh on the northern-facing slope, which we flooded, levelled, and surrounded with boards of plywood and scrap metal. There was less daylight on the northern rink, but we no longer coughed up bubbles of black after every scrimmage.

The rink was regulation-size, so Sisters Barbara and Francine fanned out—skates chopping, gowns pulled tight from the stride. I triangulated, my ankle burning from Sister Dolores's slash as I squatted to stretch my stick into the passing lane. Behind me, in goal, Suzy screamed, "Let me see the shot," and her voice was tight with fear.

Sister Barbara head-faked a pass, and I lay down to block it. But she had outwitted me. She waited until I was flat and then saucered the puck over my back to Sister Francine who one-timed it—her knee falling to the ice with the force of the shot.

Rubber rang off iron, and I looked over my shoulder to see the puck spinning in the back of the net. Sister Francine, ever-faithful to her vow of silence, opened her mouth wide in muted celebration.

Suzy, who was split-legged across the crease, uprighted. Even though she had her mask on, I knew she was furious. "Matthias!" she hollered. "Do you know what a cock-shiting line change is?"

If anyone sought to test the limits of the decree that there were no sins on the rink, it was Suzy. Off ice, we weren't allowed to even mention genitalia unless we were inside Sister Esther's first-aid room with the door latched.

Suzy whipped off her catcher (a Vaughn Pro Elite with a double-laced pocket) to hold the shaft of her goalie stick with her bare hand and blocker, as she swung it overtop the crossbar, and the paddle exploded into splinters. A Bauer 9000 with an aspen core. This was why we were not allowed to use the good sticks.

The Sisters group-hugged in celebration. Mother Superior Pamela, who was serving two minutes for hooking, hopped over the boards. "You know the rules," she said. "Five point lead and we call it. That's 6-1 by my count."

Sister Jillian let loose a *whoop-whoop* as Sister Francine soundlessly raised the roof.

"Now," Mother Superior Pamela said, "chores."

It was the end of the month's rotation. I was on Chamber Scrub and had left my cleaning supplies in the Velvet Room. Like all Chambers, the Velvet was made of concrete. It took its name from Oscar Velvet, the third astrologist to see the Kingdom of Heaven. There had been only twelve people to glimpse the jasmine city firsthand through a telescope—something about the time, light, and solar flares needing to align just so. Suzy once told me that twelve was the same number of men who had walked on the moon.

"And just like them," she said, "nobody remembers past the first three." She was rubbing mink oil into the palm of her catcher. Her hands—bruised, calloused, swollen at the knuckle—shone wet as she traced her fingers along the black scars that the puck had left on the white leather. She said, "Not that anyone needs to remember anything anymore."

I said, "You talk like an old person."

"You skate like one," she replied.

But I can name all twelve astrologists. It'd be hard not to when each of our twelve Chambers had been named after one. Nason Jr was obviously the most requested. Standing Bear and Velvet get their share of action too, having partnered to take that famous photograph of the purple dots filtering through the green walls.

But because of the dwindling numbers of pilgrims, we had all but boarded up rooms six through twelve. After the game, Sister Dolores told me to dust (can you believe that? *dust!*) Hodgeson and Curlew-Haskins. "Like," I asked, "with a feather?"

"So you're the Prince of Egypt now?" she said. "Use a rag."

Instead, I left my supplies in the Velvet, found some charcoal by the incinerator, and drew the outline of a net onto Hodgeson's concrete wall and spent the afternoon practising my wrist shot.

Then, lunch.

O'Bryan said the numbers hadn't always been so low. "There were years," he told us in the cafeteria, "when entire shanty towns were built at the base of the mountain. Thousands of pilgrims. Millions. All waiting for us."

Later, as we washed our plates, I asked Suzy what a shanty town was.

"It's a town that people shat in," she said, "because the toilets didn't work. But they weren't going to be there for long, so it didn't matter."

"Does that mean we live in a shanty town? Because of the outhouses?"

"No," she said. "Because we're here for a long time."

It was always hard to know if O'Bryan was telling the truth. The snow had erased any evidence of these makeshift cities. And just the thought of pilgrims waiting for us instead of the other way around seemed so opposite from our lives as to be impossible. Now, whenever one showed up, they walked to the front desk, signed the guest book, and Ascended the same day—same hour, even. They still brought their prized possessions to offer the Convent of the Sisters of Perpetual Mercy as a final gesture of forsaking all earthly ills, but the only people still out there were reformed conspiracy theorists—those who thought it was all a big hoax and had been living in a bomb shelter for the past twenty-five years. I could tell this by their offerings: a lot of canned goods and board games. But it was no biggie. There was enough stuff from the boom years to replace what snapped beyond repair, and most folks still managed to bring at least one piece of quality equipment or, barring that, sock tape.

Even within my lifetime, my thirteen years, I had seen the numbers plummet. There were some weeks, we didn't have any pilgrims at all. A few years previous, during a month of blizzards, two entire weeks went by without a single Ascension. Fourteen days of staying up late, of afternoon naps, of playing three full periods without interruption. Fourteen days of not seeing the upturned eyes, misty with hope, all holier-than-thou as they welcomed themselves into the Kingdom and we were left to wiggle out the axe and scrub the walls. Fourteen days of gales blowing away the smoke, of wind whistling through the dorm room's boarded-up windows like a lullaby, of waking to a world so white it was pure light.

The vuvuzela sounded, and we stirred from our bunks. School usually started at sunrise, but the smoke had returned with such a vengeance that there was confusion as to when sunrise actually began. The light was dull but constant. Even at night, there was a greyness, a glow trapped in the clouds, held over from the day.

We yawned and stretched, scratched the lice from our long johns. The floor was cold and hurt to stand on, so we hotfooted our way to the potbelly stove. Suzy and Eric would chip the skin of ice that had grown across the casserole dish while Carl B and Carl M held kindling at the ready as O'Bryan opened the stove's cast-iron door and exhaled into last night's embers. When Suzy and Eric had got through the ice (delicate, so as not to splash), they tossed the shards onto the stovetop to see when the metal grew hot. The fire crackled, the ice sizzled, and we were all pleased with each other's company. O'Bryan placed the casserole dish on the stovetop, using a laptop as a lid. I draped some facecloths above the stove, and as we waited for the water to boil, I slid open the ash trap and carefully scooped last night's cinders into a Tupperware. We were to use only inside-ash for our soap and not outside-ash because outside-ash, Sister Jillian had said, contained micro-crystal carcinogens that dried out her skin. When the water boiled, O'Bryan removed the laptop and the steam rose into the facecloths. The clothes grew damp and hot, and we peeled off our long johns to scrub our skin. Suzy turned and I washed her back—shoulder blades to tail bone. Then, she did mine. The vuvuzela sounded again. We buckled into our snow suits and filed to class.

We were waiting in our desks when Sister Adelaide entered. Major disappointment. Sister Adelaide was Sister Barbara's second-string, both as a teacher and left-winger. Sister Barbara let us papier-mâché extinct animals and construct cardboard models of bygone skylines while we nibbled gingersnaps that she'd baked in the shape of pucks. Sister Adelaide gave pop quizzes, forbade doodling, and always said, "Settle down, you little sinners," even when we weren't doing anything.

"Settle down, you little sinners," she said, and then, without a shard of ceremony, added, "Sister Barbara Ascended last night."

The whole class gasped. Sister Barbara was the youngest nun there, still had all her teeth, and the fact that she Ascended unaided cast great doubt onto the health of the other nuns.

"She left us peacefully, in her sleep, surrounded by those she loved."

From the back row, Eric raised his hand. "What Ascended her?"

Sister Adelaide said that Sister Esther believed it was an undiagnosed lung infection. Something to do with the smoke. But before Eric could ask more, we were instructed to clear off our desks and write out the multiplication tables of eighteen through forty-eight. "In pen," Sister Adelaide said, "so I know when you have erred."

We took out our ballpoints and rolled them between our palms to warm the ink.

Sister Barbara was a lethal left-winger. With her Ascension, there were only ten nuns left. Yesterday, they had two full lines and a goalie. Now, a nun would have to double-shift. We still had thirteen players—two full lines, a goalie, a backup (Carl C who was barely old enough to skate) and an extra player for the injury roster (Matthias had been subbing for Simon and his bum foot the past week and our forecheck had never been weaker).

The ink warmed, and I divided my sheet into cells and started from the top—18, 36, 52—but my heart wasn't in it. My heart was on the rink, brainstorming plays that cycled the puck through the offensive zone, the perfect attack against a tired line.

I glanced over at Suzy's sheet and saw that she was already working her way through the thirty-eights: 630, 648, 666. Funny to think that these numbers once meant something. Amazing, really, the barbarity of the past.

Lunchtime, and the cafeteria crackled with rumour.

"The story doesn't make sense," Eric said. "Why was Sister Barbara surrounded by loved ones if she didn't know about her lungs?"

Ronald said, "She was playing hard yesterday."

O'Bryan said he heard that she'd welcomed the Ascension, and Jason agreed, and Leonard said she spontaneously combusted.

"I bet she Ran Away."

Everyone shut right up. Mouths agape. We turned to Suzy.

"What?" she said, slicing her circle of canned pineapple.

Running Away would be the equivalent of suicide. And nothing cruds up the soul more than suicide, filling it with so much silt that it couldn't pass through a cheese grater, let alone the jasmine walls of the Kingdom of Heaven. But it wasn't just the act itself that was bad. It was that you couldn't be forgiven after you did it—that the ordained didn't have a chance to Bless your soul before it began its long and lumbering journey.

"I hate this canned shit," Suzy said, shoving her bowl. "And don't tell me those fister Sisters aren't hoarding the frozen pizzas."

"You know," Matthias told her, forking her pineapple into his own bowl, "each swear you speak pollutes your soul."

"And your life pollutes the planet," she replied, shoving back her chair and leaving.

"Someone's bearing the burden of Eve," Matthias said.

O'Bryan charley-horsed him in the thigh and told him to shut the fucktard up. Nobody could fault her for being on edge. Once the nuns were gone, there would be no one qualified to give the final Blessing, and Suzy—more than any of us—was concerned that the Sisters weren't going to take her topside with them.

For the nuns to take us topside, we needed to have lived without sin. But Suzy had let her temper slip a couple times, though nobody was sure if—during such moments of rage—any nun had seen. It wasn't a sin if an adult didn't witness it. Usually, the Sisters saw only the aftermath of Suzy's anger: a screwdriver plugged to its hilt into the outhouse door, a pepper grinder stomped to pieces, the potbelly stove wrenched from the chimney pipe and toppled onto its side. Fifteen years old, but Suzy had the strength of a volcano, one that had lived since the birth of the world.

Matthias, however, was adamant that the last time Suzy went molten (two or three months ago), Mother Superior Pamela had watched it all from the workshop. But it was Matthias's favourite axe handle that Suzy had busted, and we figured this was just his way of getting back at her any way he could. But if Mother Superior Pamela had indeed seen her, saw the handle split like cardboard across her thigh, Suzy could be refused the Blessing while all the rest of us Ascended, happy and whole. And she would be forced to make the forty-day trek to that abandoned military bunker in Colorado where no one knew what she had done. Of course, all of this could be averted if Suzy simply confessed to her sins, but she maintained that she would "rather die."

As we finished our pineapple, O'Bryan told us a story of a convent on the northern coast of Seattle and how all the nuns had gone topside at the same time, having fallen through the sea ice. Once there were no adults left, the kids proceeded to do horrendous, tragic, ghastly things, things that would be unspeakable if O'Bryan didn't love to speak.

"They skinned each other and sewed their flesh into capes. They cut off their own feet to use as oven mitts. One cracked open another's breathing chest to see if he could spot the soul."

Never mind that none of this made sense. Why would they want capes? Those would be terrible oven mitts. And everyone knew the soul can be seen only after it mixes with the ether of space, turning that singular shade of purple. Amazing, really, what some people believe.

But the worst thing those kids did was what they didn't do: in the frenzy of carnage, they ignored how none of them had got a Blessing, meaning their souls—despite being child-sized— would never be lithe enough to Ascend through the jasmine walls, and so they are still out there, floating through the distant corners of darkness.

Evening, and Ronald said that Mother Superior Pamela wanted to see me. Her office was situated in what was the gift shop when the convent was an upscale hunting lodge named Valhalla. All the wallpaper had been stripped off, the carpet ripped up, the windows smashed and replaced with particleboard.

Sister Barbara once explained to our class how the world was pillaged during the Year of Last Record. But more than the collapse of governments, the widespread arson, the outbursts of cannibalism in the coastal cities of Europe, what startled me most was the looting. "Why would anyone want the wallpaper?" I asked, and our gaze turned to the barren walls, the dented drywall, the exposed studs. Sister Barbara thought for a moment. "Sometimes," she said, "when people have everything they want, they confuse that for having wanted everything." And Matthias dutifully wrote her comment down in case of a quiz.

Above the door to Mother Superior Pamela's office was a small glass window that I loved to look at. I dreamed of one day standing two chairs on top each other, just so I could touch it. Invisible but impenetrable. It's the only intact glass I've ever seen.

In her office, Mother Superior Pamela rose from her desk and gestured for me to sit on the threadbare couch against the wall, where she joined me.

"Why do you think I have called you here?" she asked.

"Because yesterday I didn't dust the Hodgeson Chamber like Sister Dolores had asked."

"Why didn't you dust the Hodgeson Chamber like Sister Dolores had asked?"

"I was practising other skills."

"And did you tell Sister Dolores that you *had* dusted the Hodgeson Chamber?"

"No," I said. "She never follows up."

Mother Superior Pamela stroked her chin. "Not a sin *per se*, but just to be sure this doesn't fall under sloth, take an extra shift collecting firewood tomorrow morning."

I slumped into the cushions, and Mother Superior Pamela's face softened.

"Listen," she said, her hand on mine. "Sister Adelaide told me you were distraught upon news of Sister Barbara's Ascension. She said that you 'emotionally and intellectually withdrew' from the lesson."

"Sister Adelaide is very observant," I replied.

For awhile, we both just stared at each other.

"Tell me," Mother Superior Pamela said, "are you worried for when the Sisters Ascend?"

Truth be told, I had been making a concentrated effort to not think about this. Not because I was scared like Suzy, or impatient like Eric, but because if they Ascended without us winning a single game, that loss would sit on my soul for eternity.

Mother Superior Pamela was expecting an answer, so I defaulted to what I always said when I wasn't sure. "I'm praying on it."

She nodded and rose to her desk where she opened the top drawer. From it, she pulled a crowbar.

I thought to myself, *I will suffer like a hero*. Head-hung, I trudged to her desk and fanned my fingers across the wood.

Mother Superior Pamela rolled her eyes. "You can't believe everything O'Bryan tells you."

She turned to the boarded-up window and, with unthinking familiarity, popped off the plywood. Smoke poured in, and she flapped her long sleeves—the smoke tumbling around the black fabric—until she had banished it back over the sill.

There were two layers of smoke: the first, high above us, blotted out the sky. The second layer, below us, covered the flatlands. The only evidence there was anything else to the world aside from our mountaintop was that through the second layer of smoke, the one that encircled us like a moat, were spots of orange far beneath, breathing in and out. The flames could not always be seen so clearly, but that night's breeze had blown life into the blaze.

"How long have the fires been going?" I asked.

"About twenty years now."

"That's so long," I said.

"There is a lot of civilization to burn."

Mother Superior Pamela turned to me, looked into my eyes, and waited for me to say something.

"I'm praying on it."

She said we should meet again tomorrow. I was dismissed.

By the time I tucked myself in, I thought she was asleep. But Suzy's voice came from the top bunk like the first flakes of snow. "What do you think it will be like? The Kingdom of Heaven?"

"I dunno," I said, but of course I knew:

Silence. A pause on the inhale, and then the crack of ice taking your weight. The first strides, the squeeze of the blades around the corners. White lights overhead, and the air—crisp and clean—gathering in the pockets of your lungs as you charge overtop the blue line, painted so straight that there is never any debate between what is and is not offside.

I asked Suzy what she thought.

"The same as here," she said, and then added, "but warm. Hot. Like the feel on your face when you open the incinerator. We'll go outside in T-shirts and dresses and the sun will never leave."

"What about hockey?"

"We won't have the time," she said. "We'll be too busy being happy."

The sun had yet to rise when I tobogganed down the mountain's southern slope, stopping at the trunk of a felled tree. The wood was dry and broke like bone, so I was able to fill the sled before the smoke raked-out my throat.

As I grabbed the towrope to drag my haul back home, the wind shifted, and the smoke swirled down the slope to reveal more of the mountain than I'd ever seen. Not that there was anything to see: just some warped trees, drifts of snow and ash, the slope steepening the further it went. But just the fact that it existed—that there was so much more than what we could see, just like the nuns had promised—was nothing short of thrilling.

The slope pulled me downwards, gravity urging me towards another life. And I felt my boots follow, one after the another. And with each stride, I felt a small shock that I was actually leaving, that it was not just physically possible but (how to say this?) mentally, as well.

And I would've seen it through, if not for the doe. She appeared from between a tree that had split lengthwise during a night so cold the trunk had burst. The smoke parted around her, and her nostrils twitched as the two of us stood locked in eye contact. But then the snow beneath me shifted and I lurched forward, and when I looked up, her tracks showed that she'd fled down the mountain. But the thought of what awaited me in that grey unknown—wild and ravenous—turned me uphill, where I trudged with my toboggan back to the woodshed.

As promised, Suzy, O'Bryan, Eric, and the twins, Leonard and Percy, were waiting. I wanted the deer to be mine alone—just for awhile—so didn't say anything. We played three-on-three, no goalies, hit the post to score. The puck disappeared beneath the smoke, so we played half-rink and kept the passes short. Suzy called a time-out when she spotted the kerosene lantern descending the stairs. It was Sister Dolores, and my heart sank.

"A pilgrim has arrived," she said to me.

"Can't Matthias do it?" I asked. "He's probably just reading."

"You are on duty."

"It's a tie game," I pleaded.

"I'm sorry," she said, "but you are confusing me for someone who cares."

"Please."

"You have to the count of one." She paused. "One."

I skated to the boards and hopped over, but it was a move I had not yet perfected, and my shin pad caught on the wood's edge and swung me into the ground. Embarrassed and exhausted, I picked up my stick and swung it like an axe onto the boards.

Sister Dolores swivelled around, her eyes wild with fury. "You are not on the rink!"

From behind me, Suzy said, "It's how we get warmed up, ma'am."

Sister Dolores considered this and nodded, then continued her ascent. I clipped on my blade guards and clopped along behind.

Sister Adelaide handed us back our exam on the finer points of English grammar. "It appears," she said, "that Sister Barbara's education did not extend beyond arts and crafts."

The top of my page was marked 3/10. I looked over at Eric who had 4.5/10. O'Bryan, somehow, got -1. Suzy was covering her sheet with her hands, which meant she got perfect.

Heads down and notebooks out, we were correcting our mistakes when we heard ripping paper. Sister Adelaide was at the Wall of Fame, where Sister Barbara had hung the class's best art projects. For our snowflake project, Sister Barbara (in what turned out to be her last act as our teacher) had been so impressed that *all* of our snowflakes made the Wall. Now, Sister Adelaide was tearing them down, one-by-one.

She felt our eyes upon her, and without looking back, said, "If you want to look at snowflakes"—she ripped down Carl C's snowflake (the first time he'd ever made the Wall)—"you can go outside."

O'Bryan took this as a genuine offer and stood up. Sister Adelaide turned around and recoiled at his insolence. "Do you have any idea," she said, "how embarrassing it would be for me if you were to get into the Kingdom of Heaven? Everyone would say, 'Sister Adelaide, what have you done?' And I would be forced to answer, 'It is more a matter of what I haven't done.' And that is teach you anything."

She made O'Bryan stand at the front of the class, drop his snow pants to reveal his ice-white bum, and bend over. She began searching her desk for the rod—a taped-up set of venetian blinds—not knowing that Sister Barbara had thrown it into the furnace the same day Sister Adelaide had dropped it off. As O'Bryan waited, bent at the waist and trying to hide the smile from his face, Sister Adelaide ransacked the drawers, slamming them open and closed, catching her black sleeves, searching for what was not there.

"And your chores? You're in the Betterment phase, yes?"

"I'm on Ascensions. I was Betterment two rotations ago."

"I always confuse you and Suzy," Mother Superior Pamela said, palming her forehead. She asked what I had bettered two rotations ago.

"I mended the roping on the nets and repainted the red line and face-off dots."

She frowned. "Seems a bit small for a month's work."

"Everyone's so protective about their shoelaces," I said, "that I had to fix the nets using plastic clips from bread bags that I melted with a barbecue lighter. And for the lines, I had to thaw the ice with heated-up skillets and then pry the painted planks from the marsh, and Sister Harriette made me use nail polish for paint because wastefulness is gracelessness."

Mother Superior Pamela chuckled. "Why so many pilgrims give us cosmetics will forever astound me."

"And I can only work between games," I added, but she held up her hand.

"You know," she said, "you can work on something other than the rink. Matthias re-stuffed the Sisters' mattresses with shredded tote bags."

"He is an inspiration," I said.

"And last month," she said, "you were on Chamber Scrub, yes? I hear some dislike that phase the most. The smell, I suppose."

I nodded.

"So you're on Ascensions now?"

I nodded.

"Is it hard?"

I nodded.

"And you understand why the Sisters cannot help?"

I nodded.

"Because what you're doing is a sin," she said, explaining it anyway. "Not a bad one, mind you. Nothing you can't confess and be absolved of later. But when we confirm someone's sinlessness, we ourselves must be unblemished."

I could tell by the quieting of her voice that she had begun to forget I was there.

"But who knows what is forgivable and unforgivable? A white lie may be fine by itself, but might change depending on what you're lying about. Take, for example, if you children were to engage in lust."

I gasped, disgusted.

"I know, I know," she said. "But just an example. Suddenly, the white lie burns itself red."

I hid the blush of my cheeks by staring at the threadbare cushions and pinch the ash off them.

"Or, another example," she said, "if you were to Run Away," she said. "Is it really so bad? To throw yourself upon the mercy of the world."

This question, which begged so obvious an answer, seemed a trap. Of course, it was bad: it is the one thing we are given, a soul. All else must be earned through struggle and sacrifice, the chipped fingernails of scrubbing concrete clean. Just to think about it gave me goosebumps: to not cherish your life but let it tumble down the slope into the ash and fire. For if we were to cast ourselves out from the mountain, down into the flatland flames below, we would be throwing ourselves into Hell. It is why, out of all the terrible things we did to each other (the beatings and the bullyings, the stolen clothes and skate laces, the time we bungee-chorded Matthias naked to a tree and slapshotted snowballs at him), we never even joked about Running Away. And when O'Bryan whispered of the one kid who had—he said—Ran Away, he did so with deep solemnity.

A knock at the door. Sister Dolores.

"Mother Superior," she said, "a pilgrim has arrived and the child"—she nodded at me—"is on shift."

"We are having a conversation," Mother Superior Pamela replied. "Someone can cover."

Sister Dolores frowned. "Unfortunately not. The other two are waylaid. Carl C has the flu, and Simon's severed toe still hasn't healed."

"Is it infected?"

"Sister Esther says only because he's been picking it."

Mother Superior Pamela fidgeted with her rosary. "We get barrels of nail polish but not a single pair of steel-toed boots."

"Matthias can do it," I said.

Sister Dolores ignored me until she saw that Mother Superior Pamela was waiting for a response.

"Matthias," Sister Dolores said, deepening her frown, "is currently on Chamber Scrub, so is ineligible."

This regulation, stating that someone on Ascensions was forbidden to simultaneously work Chamber Scrub, didn't always exist: the days before the chore wheel. O'Bryan said that a long time ago, a boy was sweeping up some bone shard he had just hacked free and something inside him snapped.

Sister Dolores cleared her throat, and Mother Superior Pamela looked at me. "Same time tomorrow."

Suzy had waited up for me. After I washed off my hands in the casserole dish's frigid water, I lay down and stared at the top bunk's plywood. "How many years you got left until you age out and go topside?"

"Two," Suzy answered. "O'Bryan's only got six months, the lucky ball-biter."

"One? I thought he was just a couple months older than you."

"I thought so too, but Sister Martha told him the other day that he's *seventeen*, and in under a year...," she snapped her fingers and whistled a long, fading note.

I felt a sudden pang of sadness, that between Suzy's two and O'Bryan's one, my four seemed an eternity. I was about to tell Suzy this, but she said, "When kids go topside, how sure are you that the Sisters are actually Blessing them?"

"What do you mean?" I said. "You saw Kendra's Ascension."

Sometime last year, Sister Martha fetched Kendra (our best defenceman) from the cafeteria, telling her she turned eighteen that morning. Kendra insisted that her and Suzy and had been taken in the same week, but Sister Martha assured them this was only gossip. "Our records don't lie," she said, and told Kendra to choose someone to free her soul from her body. Kendra chose Suzy, and as I watched the two walk out the cafeteria, I felt a shameful sense of glee, knowing that once Kendra was gone, Suzy would have no other choice but to love me as much as I loved her. We played a defenceman short until Carl C finally got good enough at skating backwards to be drafted.

"When Kenny Ascended," Suzy said to me, and then trailed off for so long I thought she'd fallen asleep. "It's hard to explain, but it was like—*nothing*. Nothing happened. She just lay there, slumped, and Sister Dolores went to find out who was on Chamber Scrub and asked me to light the incinerator on my way back."

Every kid had performed Ascensions, but there were only a handful who had performed them on a friend. And now that Suzy mentioned it, there *was* something different about those who had: O'Bryan with Reggie, Eric with Graham, Percy with whatever that really tall kid's name was, and Suzy with Kendra. It was like something had been carved out of them in the Chamber, something that they didn't know was there until it was gone.

"Hurry the fucktard up," O'Bryan told us as Eric wedged the bellows into the incinerator's porthole and pumped. The flames roared, fuelled by the family of five that Leonard had found frozen on the mountainside that morning when he was collecting firewood. So close but so far.

O'Bryan tossed a snowball onto the incinerator's flattop, and the snow sizzled into a puddle. The heat had finally arrived, and we slid our pots of snow onto the flattop and waited with forced casualness, looking over our shoulders to see if any Sisters approached. The good pots were to not leave the cafeteria.

The lids began to clatter, O'Bryan called places, and everyone formed a bucket-brigade. Wearing my leather mitts, I passed a pot to Leonard who passed it to Simon who passed it to Jason to Suzy, then Carl C, and then Ronald, who passed it to either Carl B or Carl M, who were straddling the rink's boards. The Carls threw the water across the ice, where Matthias—the zamboni—was on his shin pads and holding a windshield wiper in each hand, which he used to spread the water before it froze. If Matthias didn't spread the water quick enough, it froze uneven and one of the Carls would make him use his bare hands to smooth-out the blotches. That day, the temperature dipped below thirty, and the water thickened the instant it touched the ice. But a five-person incinerator was an opportunity not to be missed.

Empty pots were ferried back, which O'Bryan and Eric hard-packed with snow and returned to the incinerator's top. As I rotated off the boiling pots, I looked down the hillside, towards the sound of laughter. Matthias scurried around the home team's goal line as Carl B and Carl M threw pots of water in alternating corners. Matthias slid into one corner to smooth the surface, only for Carl M to throw a pot in the opposite direction. Matthias's mistake was not that he moved too slow but too fast, splashing water onto his mitts, which started to grow columns of ice reaching up his arms.

I turned back to my pots clattering happily. I passed one to Leonard and saw Matthias dashing back and forth, his mitts now solid white, as the Carls taunted. Carl B threw a bucket out to the blue line, and the spiral of water corkscrewed through the air like a great snake, steam rising from it, until it shattered over the ice. Matthias scrambled to the blue line as Carl M dumped a bucket over the crease and hollered for Matthias's attention. Matthias pivoted and ran towards the crease but slipped and fell backwards, smacking the toque off his head. But then, Carl B threw another pot towards the blue line. And Matthias sat up and caught the scalding water in his face.

The part I will remember most is not the sound of his screams, or the uselessness of his ice-block hands grabbing at his face, or even the shocked stillness with which we all watched. The part I will remember most is how his cheek kept sticking to ice and how his whole body had to thrash to tear it free.

Suzy sprinted the steps, three at a time, shoving kids out the way until she was at the boards, hopped over, grabbed him by the shoulders, and dragged his kicking body through the home team's entrance, to a snowbank, where she shoved his face in, keeping her hand rigid on the crown of his head.

The snowbank muffled Matthias's screams. We closed in like ghosts. When Matthias had gone quiet, Suzy pulled him free, his face the colour of chapped lips.

"I can't see," he said. And at first I thought he'd gone blind because his eyes were two white orbs. But they were blocks of ice. Suzy took a deep snort, all the way to her throat, and spat a glob into each of them. She shook off her gloves and rubbed in the spit, unfreezing his eyes open.

Those white orbs changed what I believed about us, what we would do if left to our own devices, how the violence we would surely visit upon each other would be limited not to the rink but the entire world. And all that held us back was the thin curtain of black that hung from each head of the Sisters of Perpetual Mercy.

"Do you see?" I asked no one and everyone. "Do you see how much we need them?"

That night, I told Suzy to *shh*. "Do you hear that?" I whispered to the underside of her bunk.

"Hear what?"

"*Shh*."

Outside, the wind groaned. The stove pinged, shrinking from hot to cold. O'Bryan snored.

"Never mind," I said.

"What did you think you heard?"

"Something in the snow."

Above me, Suzy's bed creaked as she shifted onto her side to go to sleep. "Who'd be outside at this hour?"

The next morning, a Sunday, I skipped morning scrimmage to search outside for hoof prints.

But there had been flurries overnight and according to the uniform blanket of the snow, not a single thing—not even ourselves—existed.

Weeks passed, Matthias's face healed, but his hands remained frostbit and warped. Sister Esther wouldn't pardon him from chores unless he stopped playing hockey, saying if he could grip a stick, he could grip a broom. But he refused to surrender his skates.

The snow fell without stopping, and each night, I listened to the flurries hiss into the flatland's flames. The fires were far too large to be doused, so the blizzards only thickened the smoke.

Some mornings, we had to tie scarves around our faces and the nuns folded their habits' wings across their mouths.

When pilgrims arrived, they emerged from the smoke like ghosts. It wasn't until Sister Jillian summoned them to stand before the check-in desk, that we got a good look.

"We heard this is how you pass the time," said a man in black-and-white camouflage. Sister Jillian accepted the four pairs of shin pads—Warrior Ultralites with a flex knee, never been worn, sizes s through XL. The shin pads shone like the top fat on canned coconut milk.

The woman he was with (also in camo) emptied the large backpack carrying the rest of their offering: forty cans of sweet corn, a ten-kilo sack of oatmeal, five jugs of almond milk, and two tubes of mascara. She nuzzled her head against the man's bearded neck. "I wonder how we will pass the time up there."

"Barf," said Ronald.

Sister Jillian shot him a glare that could crack concrete, and he went back to dragging his whetstone across the blade. I returned to sweeping.

As the path up the mountain had become overgrown, the offerings had decreased.

"There's more," the man said as he signed the guest book, "but we had to leave it at the second set of caves. Canned tomatoes, some ratchets, a laundry rack. Maybe some of the rug rats can fetch it."

But before I could volunteer, Sister Jillian held up her hand. "Absolutely not." She returned to the shin pads. "These are more than generous." She traced her finger against the ribbed plastic until the woman cleared her throat.

"Ronald," Sister Jillian said to her, "will take you to the Van Dousselle room and, sir—," she flipped a page in her ledger,

"—we have an opening in the Sanford room. Sister Dolores and Sister Nicola shall offer the Blessings today."

"We were hoping we could be together," the man said.

"Only one pilgrim per room," Sister Jillian replied. "Fewer cold feet."

"Could I get the Standing Bear room?" the woman asked. "It's just, I've always been a fan."

Sister Jillian consulted her ledger—which, unbeknownst to the couple, was empty aside from her drawings of goalie mask designs. She hummed and hawed and flipped a couple pages, the pleats of her sleeves swishing across the paper. "I suppose I must move some things around."

She snapped her fingers and Ronald rose, standing like an old person, pushing off with his hands against his knees. He slung the axe handle over his shoulder and led them down the hallway. "Do either of you have to use the bathroom?" he asked. "Makes it easier on us."

I swooped in for the shin pads in a size M, but Sister Jillian snatched them back and etched her name on the front.

At supper, as we sipped on our cans of sweet corn, I was telling everyone who'd listen about the shin pads when Eric interrupted: "Does it strike anyone as odd that pilgrims know we play hockey?"

"Why wouldn't they know that?" Percy asked.

Eric squinted with disappointment. "Who would've told them, Percy?"

Mother Superior Pamela entered the cafeteria and spoke with Sisters Harriette and Philomena in hushed tones.

"O'Bryan," Eric said, leaning in. "What was the name of that kid who Ran Away?"

"Joshua."

"And did Joshua—?"

The three nuns rushed past, their gowns catching the wind.

We were alone in the cafeteria, but Eric still whispered. "Did Joshua play hockey?"

O'Bryan's face turned a holy kind of white. "He was the one who made the first rink, on the eastern plateau. Before the fires."

School the next morning, and Sister Adelaide told us Sister Nicola has Ascended. "Along with Sister Dolores."

"Are you serious?" Eric said.

I expected Sister Adelaide to mock him, but instead, she softened her eyes. "Yes, child. I am serious." Then, to the class: "Late last night, surrounded by those they loved the most. Sister Esther believes it to be a lung condition."

"For both?" asked Eric.

Sister Adelaide said he'd have to ask Sister Esther.

"Sister Adelaide?" Suzy said from the back row. "Should we pray for them?"

Sister Adelaide's true self returned: her eyes sharpened, her jaw set, her mouth frowned. "Pray for yourselves," she said, "you little sinners."

That night, we were lucky and the nuns joined us.

The smoke grew even thicker, so Mother Superior Pamela allowed us to use the battery-operated headlamps: ours were red, the nuns', white.

In the low visibility, it was hard to establish an attack, and the nuns scored only once in the first period, a tipped shot from the point. By the beginning of the second, we could barely see the ice beneath us, just the headlamps gliding. There was a scrum in front of the nuns' crease, and I watched from the hash marks as the lights tangled and fell until Jason shouted, "It's in! It's in!"

For the first time I could remember, we had tied the game.

"We're going to do it," Suzy told us, breathless, as we huddled at our bench during the last intermission. "We are going to play three full periods."

At their bench, the Sisters were silhouettes, hovering. With only seven players plus Sister Martha in net, they hadn't been able to change forwards, and Sisters Francine, Adelaide, and Jillian had been on-ice without rest. We could hear them sucking air and horking ash.

The logic of our penalties was we only called what a ref would've seen. And since the third period's visibility worsened to nightmarish levels, the referee would be blind as an apple, so we played no-holds barred. Through the smoke, a massacre:

Sister Francine tomahawked her stick into Leonard's shoulder. Percy defended his twin by spearing Sister Francine in the stomach, and Sister Francine—true to her vow of silence—didn't let a sound escape as she gasped for air. Sister Adelaide slew-footed Percy to the ground, elbow-dropping him in the scuffle. Next play, Sister Adelaide cut across the crease, and Suzy clotheslined her with her blocker. Later in the period, Sister Adelaide pinned me to the boards and fed me kidney shots, but I whiplashed my head and heard my helmet crack against her face. She spat at me—a hard glob hitting my cheek—before crosschecking me in the lower back and catching up with her defence. As I rose from the ice, I saw what she had horked: her tooth.

The egg timer rang and signalled the end of the third. For a beat, there was only the sound of blades on ice and the panting of a breath none of us could catch.

"What do we do now?" Leonard asked.

"Five-minute overtime," Mother Superior Pamela said, wiping a dangle of blood off her chin. "Sudden death."

At our bench, Eric urged us to play it safe and take the tie. And we were doing just that, until with ninety seconds left, Sister Harriette broke her stick on a slash across Ronald's forearm and, with their best defenceman hobbled, we ratcheted up the pressure.

I was on the blue line, watching the puck thread through the smoke as we cycled the play. I could tell by the angle of the headlights where the puck slid and was ready for it as it darted towards me. I caught it in my skates, and I looked up to see the white light of a nun, charging. I could either retreat from the hit or make the pass.

How many times in your life do you get a chance to be the absolute best version of yourself? Four, maybe five? And then, too, there are the opportunities, even rarer, to be even *better* than that version, to corral a courage you know you cannot sustain but can hold for a flash because you also know it's just a little bit of pain and the worst is already over.

I kicked the puck onto my stick and passed to Matthias whose red light shone farther down the blue line. The puck departed into the smoke as my red headlight illuminated the two metre, 110 kilogram silhouette of Sister Philomena. And everything turned slow-motion as my body departed from the ice.

I hovered in the air, untouched by gravity, and all existence faded beneath me: the rink, the boards, the frozen marsh. Then went the outhouses, the convent, the Chambers. The red and white headlamps become distant candles as the mountain, the fires, the entire world fell away. And I rose into the night sky, above the ceiling of smoke, to see the stars, and they looked exactly like what Sister Barbara had promised. "People used to see these?" Suzy had asked her. "Every night?"

"Except," Sister Barbara had said, "when there was a moon."

I passed asteroids and planets and the swirling border of our galaxy. And it was very dark for a very long time.

But then, a green dot. It grew larger and larger, until it became a single wall that blocked the rest of infinity. And then I heard it: on the other side of the wall, a woman crying.

She was explaining how sorry she was that she Ascended by herself, that she should have waited, that all she wanted was a clean soul. The sound was so helpless that I tried to pass through the wall and threw myself against the jasmine. But I bounced back, and since there was nothing to hold on to, I floated—helplessly, slowly, back to where Earth awaited.

And as I floated further, the crying grew frantic, desperate, unhinged and animal, as if the woman could feel me leaving. The wall shrank from sight as I drifted back towards the galaxy's outer rim, and just before the crying quieted completely, I felt the word in my mouth even though I did not know how it got there:

"Mother."

"Pardon?" Mother Superior Pamela said from her desk. She was eating a jar of frozen blood.

"Oh, this?" she said catching my stare. "This was Sister Martha's idea. Something to use all that maraschino juice. It's called a snow cone."

I was on her couch with a wool blanket over me. My equipment had been removed, and I was wearing my long johns.

"The fire had gone out in the infirmary," she said, "so I told Sister Esther to put you here. She said it's nothing to be worried about, that you'll just have a headache for a couple days."

"Did we win?" I asked in a voice that sounded deep and dry.

She scraped the bottom of the jar with her spoon. "Afraid not. Matthias bobbled your pass, and Sister Francine went five-hole on the breakaway."

I sat upright on the couch beside her, and the room wobbled. "There wasn't a penalty on Sister Philomena?"

"For what?"

"Charging."

"She says she never left her feet."

"Boarding."

"It was open ice."

"Unsportsmanlike?"

She wiped the red off her lips with her sleeve. "There, you may have a point."

She walked to me and held open my eyelids to check my irises. "It's good you woke up," she said. "I got to thinking that you'd do anything to get out of these meetings."

If I had thought that getting battering-rammed by Sister Philomena would have got me out of these meetings, I would have stick handled with my head down a long time ago.

Just before the night's game, O'Bryan and Eric cornered me in the changing shed.

"What are you telling Mother Superior?" Eric asked.

"Nothing," I replied, which was basically true. Mother Superior Pamela would ask me about school or Suzy or chores, and whatever my response, she would nod her head, her eyes fixed so intently upon me that I got the impression my responses answered much more than her questions asked.

"If you're not talking about anything important" Eric said, "maybe you should start."

"What do you mean?"

"Like why all the nuns are Ascending."

I said okay, and Eric slapped me lightly on the cheek. "And listen to me," he said, pressing his finger against my chest. "If you come back taking about 'lung conditions' I will throw your fucking skates in the fire."

In Mother Superior Pamela's office, I pictured my prized CCM Tack 5s with their laces untied and tongues lolling among the femurs and jaws, and my eyes begin to water. "Why are the nuns Ascending?"

She put her hand on my shoulder. "Their lungs." And then she gestured in the air. "The smoke. The altitude."

But her answer only ached me more, and tears began to drip down my cheeks. She wiped them away with her sleeve. "We Sisters," she said, "are in a bit of a pickle. Pilgrims are few and far between. We must be almost at the end."

She began to pick her fingernails, and against the black of her gown, her hands seemed white to the point of death. "And how long will the food last? And when will the fires climb up the mountain?" She was now speaking only to her hands. "And what happens if someone arrives with no intention of being Blessed?"

She remembered I was there. "It's just…" she said, and forced a smile. "Well, you've seen the pictures. The Kingdom is so far away." She inhaled through her nose, exhaled out her mouth. "Sometimes, I think it would've been better if we had all laicized during the Year of Last Record. Like the priests."

"What's a priest?"

She asked, "You know how we can only Bless people because we ourselves are free of sin?"

I nodded.

"But what happens when there is no one left to Bless, and to live *requires* sin?"

I shrugged. "We can Bless you."

She looked at me with a look of surprise and pity, of fear and disgust. But as quickly as it came, the look vanished, and I was dismissed.

Outside her office and at the end of the hall, Eric and O'Bryan were waiting. Suzy was with them too but was facing away as she sanded down the hallway's exposed studs to prevent slivers—the final stage of her Betterment project.

"So?" Eric asked. "Why are the nuns Ascending?"

A headache clawed at the back of my eyes. "I think," I said, "the nuns are Running Away."

Suzy turned and looked at me. I could tell by her eyes that she'd been crying.

"Why?" asked Eric.

"To join a convent in Arkansas, where there are still pilgrims."

"Why is she telling you this?"

"She says my mother was from Alabama and wanted to know if I knew anything about the convent there."

"Arkansas or Alabama?"

"Right."

"If your mom's from Alabama, why'd she come here?"

"She moved when she was eighteen because she wanted to be a farmer."

Eric took a step closer. "But you would've been too young to remember anything your mom said. That's why you're here."

I laughed. "That's what I told her!"

"And why would your mom move to the mountains to be a farmer?"

O'Bryan told Eric to give it up. "What the fucktard is this," he said, "the Spanish Infestation?" (Sister Adelaide had been lecturing on the history of Western civilization, saying Sister Barbara's lessons had been too concerned with "feeling good about ourselves.")

Eric stared at me, then clicked his tongue. "Right."

"Right," O'Bryan said, slapping me on the back. "Way to take a hit. But Matthias bobbled your pass."

"Mother Superior told me."

"But did she tell you that Percy and I duct-taped his frost-bit hands to his stick and are making him sleep like that tonight?"

I laughed again, but it made me dizzy. We heard the plodding of Sister Philomena's footsteps from the far end of the hall as she did her rounds. The four of us retreated to the dorms, and as I walked past the exposed stud, I saw that Suzy had not been finishing her Betterment project but sabotaging it. Chiselled into the wood:

WE

WERE

HERE

By morning, Sister Philomena had Ascended.

Not a single pilgrim all week.

I took to waiting at the lobby desk, sitting beside Sister Jillian and Eric (who was also on Ascensions), my hands wrung with the worry that no one else was coming, that this was the rest of our lives.

I waited past the Ascension of Sister Francine.

Not a single pilgrim the next week.

I waited past the Ascension of Sister Esther.

Not a single pilgrim the next.

Each night when I entered Mother Superior Pamela's office, I expected to see that she, too, had Ascended.

Not a single pilgrim the week after.

But Mother Superior Pamela did not Ascend.

When the two men collapsed through the lobby door, I was so happy I clapped.

"Be professional," Sister Jillian hissed.

They looked young, hardly older than O'Bryan. Both starvation-thin, and the holes of their cheekbones sunk so deep that their skulls pushed through their skin. One had a bandage wrapped around his eye, like the pirate from Sister Barbara's picture books. The other's jaw and neck had been badly burned.

"We are here," the pirate said, "to Ascend."

"Both of you?" Sister Jillian asked, and the burn man nodded.

"He can't talk," the pirate said. "Fire got into his throat."

"Not a problem," Sister Jillian said, and began to rifle through the drawers. "We had a deaf woman—years ago—in the same situation." She flitted her eyes between the men. "Well, not the *same* situation, but you understand."

She rooted around the back of a drawer. "And we found" she said, "a workaround."

In her hand, she produced a crumpled piece of paper. "A form," she said. "An affidavit." She looked at the burn man and talked at him very loudly. "WHICH YOU CAN SIGN." She mimed the gesture. Then, to the pirate: "We're almost certain the result is the same."

The pirate asked what happens if it doesn't work.

Sister Jillian laughed. "You bounce back here, I suppose."

The pirate looked over his shoulder to where Jason and Carl C were playing hockey with two brooms and an empty can of sweet corn. "Will we," he said, then cleared his throat. "Will we have to renounce each other?"

"I don't want to know," Sister Jillian said, holding up her hands. "Right now, we believe that you have not sinned and that's the way we want it." She turned to the burn man. "REGARDLESS OF YOUR FRIENDSHIP."

"Okay," the burn man croaked, and raised his hand—which I saw was also burned—to wipe away a track of water that had trickled from beneath the pirate's eye rag.

Sister Jillian snapped her fingers. Eric and I stood at attention. "Our wards will guide you to your respective Chambers where Sister Martha will offer you the Blessing. We are a bit short-staffed at the moment so—"

"The children do it?" the pirate said. "The Ascension?"

Sister Jillian cocked her head to the side. "You can't very well expect us to." She made a big show of closing her ledger. "Maybe you and your *friend* aren't right for this particular convent. Perhaps you should head to Colorado."

"No," the pirate said. "We'll never make it. Please. We just—" He glanced at Eric and me. "We don't want to go to Hell."

Sister Jillian glanced at the burn man. "Looks like you've already been."

The burn man's fingers couldn't grip the pen, so the pirate held his friend's hand and guided his signature onto the form.

"Now," Sister Jillian continued, "are there any offerings I may unburden you of?"

"We couldn't find anything," the pirate said, and Sister Jillian frowned. His voice frayed with desperation: "There's nothing left."

Eric retrieved the axes from behind the counter, and as he did, Sister Jillian hissed something in his ear.

We led the pilgrims down the hallway, and I asked him what Sister Jillian had said.

He looked over his shoulder as the two men followed us, holding hands. "She told us, Make it hurt."

Amazing, really, that she thought it needed saying.

Later that night, a thud hit the window's particleboard cover. Mother Superior Pamela and I stared at each other, unsure if the sound was only in our heads. But it happened again.

"Is that," I asked Mother Superior Pamela, "a soul returning?"

Another thud, followed by a holler.

Mother Superior Pamela rolled her eyes. "The things O'Bryan tells you."

She told me to stay put and left her office. As I waited, another thud hit the wood, and I took the crowbar from Mother Superior Pamela's desk to pry off the bottom corner of the particleboard and peek through.

A kerosene lantern had been dropped atop the crusted snow, and the flame cast a light onto the silhouette behind it. The silhouette bent over, picked up some snow, and launched another snowball against the particleboard. And then came the holler: "I know you're still woken up!"

I had heard that voice before. Many times, in fact. But now, the context was so different, I took a minute to connect it.

"I know it for a fact!"

Sister Adelaide.

She bent to pick up another snowball but lost her balance and fell face-first into a drift. "Goddammit," she said, rising.

But when she stood, there was something wrong with her legs. She swayed a bit, unsure of her footing.

From the darkness, came Mother Superior Pamela, the white trim of her habit catching the lantern's light.

"I knew you'd come outside," Sister Adelaide said. "I knew." Each word was thick, sluggish, like last year when Percy got hip-checked by Sister Philomena and clamped his teeth through his tongue and spoke like syrup for five months.

Mother Superior Pamela said something to Sister Adelaide, but Sister Adelaide grabbed her shoulders. "Do you have any idea how warm it is down there?"

The lantern, on its side, started burning spilled fuel and orange light rose beneath them.

Mother Superior Pamela said something and struggled to free herself, but Sister Adelaide held her. "Just for a stroll, Pam. Like we used to."

Their faces touched, and the lantern burned its way into the snow and was extinguished. And only for the sound of the crusted snow breaking, I knew they were still there.

It was the only time I dismissed myself to bed.

"Do you ever think what will happen to us when the Sisters go topside?"

I shrugged at Suzy and continued brushing my teeth. "We'll go topside too," I said.

"How?" Suzy said, who was flossing. "There'll be nobody to bless us."

"We'll be fine," I said, growling into the cracked mirror. "We haven't made any graven images, committed adultery, or coveted anybody's ox. The only thing that could crud up our soul is Running Away."

"You believe that?"

"Eric believes that. And that guy"—spit—"doesn't believe *anything*."

As I swirled the toothbrush in a cup of water to rinse it, I caught Suzy's reflection in the mirror. She said, "What about that time O'Bryan talked about, before the chore wheel? That kid—why did cleaning up the Chamber he'd been working make him go crazy?"

"How should I know why someone goes crazy?"

"I think that cleaning up what you've done makes you realize what you've done."

I spat. "That's what we tell Matthias when he wets the bed."

Suzy faced me. "That convent on the northern coast of Seattle," she said. "Why were the nuns all out on the sea ice together?"

My bare feet ached on the floor. The wooden boards held such coldness that I closed my eyes and imagined that I, too, was out on the sea ice, the huddle of black habits swaying nearby as the snow-driven winds erased them from sight.

"Sometimes," Suzy said, "when I'm by myself on the rink, I feel this loneliness. And the cold becomes a white echo." She rubbed her face. "I'm not afraid of it. I'm not. But I've never seen anyone else down there alone."

"What are you talking about?"

She said, "At the end of every game, someone has to be the last one on the ice."

I woke early. I pocketed some Pop-Tarts and tippy-toed out the dorm, got dressed in the hallway, and descended the southern slope, in search of the deer. I had kept the secret from Suzy but also from Mother Superior Pamela.

The Sisters were always telling us that large plans were at work and we featured as mere pieces within them. Even Sister Barbara had stressed how incredibly small we were: "No larger than a snowflake in a blizzard," she had said before instructing us on that day's art project. But out of everyone in existence, the deer had chosen me. And so who were the Sisters—who was Mother Superior Pamela—to say that I was only a lowly servant of a higher purpose, a mere henchman of divinity?

I had been searching for the deer every day since I first saw her. But the days turned into months and I never glimpsed her again (or any footprints, or scat, or tufts of hair), and I began to think that I had never actually seen her and it was just some trick of the light. If this were true and the deer was only ash and wind, then the Sisters' warnings about the allure of ego were apt and I had fallen prey to the vanity of belief—my inclination to consider myself the centre of some grand story, one that was unfolding all around me like curls of smoke leaving an ember, a story in which I would inevitably solve all the various questions that burned in my mind during those sleepless moments of predawn grey.

I arrived where I had left the Pop-Tarts the morning before, as I had been doing for weeks by then. The snacks had always been left untouched. But what did that prove?

"Those kids on the northern coast of Seattle," I asked Mother Superior Pamela. "Why were the nuns all out on the sea ice together?"

We had been talking about what I would work on during my Betterment phase now that the chore wheel had rotated, and my question caught her off guard. She said, "I can't speak for how another convent ran itself."

I expected her to chastise me for believing everything that O'Bryan said, but her dodging of the question validated it.

All that day, a sharp breeze had whisked away the smoke, and Mother Superior Pamela now pried the particleboard off her window. We gazed down the mountain at the never-ending greyness, which appeared as calm as ice.

"And the kids," I said. "Who will Bless us when all the Sisters are gone?"

Mother Superior Pamela smiled. "When we Ascend, you will get to decide that for yourselves. You will finally be in charge." And as she listed off all the fun we would have—no chores, no school, no nothing—a thought occurred to me that I never had before: *so this,* I thought, *is what it feels like to be lied to.*

"Why are we having these meetings?" I asked.

"I thought you enjoyed them," Mother Superior Pamela replied.

I didn't say anything, and the two of us were quiet for awhile. I knew if I didn't speak, she would eventually have to answer my question.

"Suzy has been Ascending the nuns," she said.

In my heart of hearts, I suppose I'd already known this but was too afraid to admit it. Over the past months, with Suzy's every look and touch and every snapped goalie stick, I had felt the shape of the secret take form. And I knew this not from deduction or reason but rather pure intuition—the way you catch a pass without looking—some combination of pace and instinct.

Mother Superior Pamela said, "Suzy and I had been meeting for months before she agreed. Sister Martha is next, and in a couple weeks, it will only be myself and Sister Adelaide. We will Bless each other simultaneously, and—" she put her hand on mine "—*simultaneously* two children will Ascend us. Then, you will be free to live how you wish."

Below us, a fuel source caught, and a fireball ripped clear above the smoke cover as large waves of orange ebbed beneath the grey.

Mother Superior Pamela said, "We asked her who she wanted to help her. And she said you."

She craned her neck out the window, looking up into the dark sky. Eric once hypothesized that the two layers of smoke was a lie—that everyone everywhere was living in the same cloud and the layers were just a mirage of perception.

Far away, a streak of purple fell through the sky, splitting into thinner lines of light before disappearing into the flatlands.

"A satellite," Mother Superior Pamela said. "They're finally starting to fall."

But I did not know what a satellite was. Nor do I know now. And it kind of hollows me out to think that I had the chance to ask but didn't—just like I'll never get the chance to touch that windowpane above Mother Superior Pamela's door. Because at that moment, my mind wasn't there. It was halfway down the southern slope. Because that was the moment I decided to Run Away.

And I would have, too. But the baby arrived.

Sister Harriette was on night shift and heard the crying. The sound came from the eastern plateau, and by the time Mother Superior Pamela and I had left her office, everyone else—both kids and nuns—had gathered at the front desk when the woman covered in towels and rain jackets finally limped though the doors while carrying a screaming swaddle in her arms.

Sister Harriette rushed to take the bundle, which the woman surrendered with exhaustion. As Sister Harriette held the lump of blankets against her chest and made little bouncing motions, we encircled her to watch the reveal of the smallest face I had ever seen.

"She's starving," Sister Martha said and told Jason to fetch a turkey baster and Carl M to warm up a glass of almond milk.

"Coconut," Sister Harriette said. "There's more fat."

Suzy wedged between Eric and Leonard to caress the baby's face with her fingertips. The baby cooed and everyone—even O'Bryan—melted. Everyone except me. I was staring at Suzy, trying harder than I've ever tried anything to get her to look at me, so I could convey all that I knew, and she could convey all that she knew, and we would both know that we were in it together.

But she did not look. Everyone had pivoted their attention to the lobby desk where the woman was letting loose a terrible moan. "Please," she said to Mother Superior Pamela, "please," and then lurched towards the baby.

Mother Superior Pamela held her by the shoulders. "I know," she said, "but if they're too young to talk, they're too young to agree to the Blessing."

"But what does she need to be Blessed for?" the woman said, struggling to get free. "She's six months."

Mother Superior Pamela told her, in a voice so full of pity it hurt, "Everyone needs to be Blessed."

The woman struggled against Mother Superior Pamela's defenceman strength, but eventually collapsed into her black gown.

"The child will be safe with us," Mother Superior Pamela said, stroking the back of her head. "We have raised many children before. Just look at them."

The woman raised her face from Mother Superior Pamela's gown. And for the first time, she really saw us, the way the deer had seen me: all thirteen kids, grubby faces, broken fingernails, black eyes and chipped teeth. Hand-me-down long johns, wool toques, slippers in the shape of claws. Bucktoothed and knock-kneed.

"Can't we just Bless her and see what happens?" the woman asked.

Sister Adelaide chuckled. "It's a long way for the soul to travel only to bounce right back."

The woman spoke so quietly it was like we were reading her mind. "Can't you make an exception?"

Mother Superior Pamela was the one to say it, but any of us could have: "There are no exceptions in the Kingdom of Heaven."

"May I have the night to think?"

"Of course. We will fix a bed for the two of you in the Hodgeson Chamber."

Sister Adelaide handed the baby back to her, and the woman wiped her nose with her hand. "May we have the Nason Jr instead? I've always been a fan."

"Of course," Mother Superior Pamela said and guided the two down the hallway.

As the rest of us headed the opposite way to the dorm, Sister Martha told Suzy to remain since she was on Ascensions and should be on standby. Sister Adelaide interrupted and said that Matthias or Leonard could do it since they were on duty too.

As the Sisters argued back and forth, it happened: I met Suzy's eyes. *I know*, I mouthed. Her face twisted but then relaxed, and I felt all that was unsaid pass between us.

"It's okay," Suzy said, and I was about to say that I disagreed, that our futures seemed sealed with suffering, that disaster was breaking like an avalanche, but I realized she was not talking to me.

Sisters Adelaide and Martha looked at her.

"I want to do it," she said.

Back in the dorm, everyone was talking about the baby and woman. And I knew that I should tell them what I had learned, but how could I explain that Suzy had known for months but hadn't said anything? They were going to burn my skates for keeping quiet about information that I didn't even know. What would they burn of hers for keeping quiet about our entire lives?

A secret always seems so easy to get rid of—but when you have it, how quickly you love its weight, how it glides with you wherever you go and fills you with a worth you didn't think you had. But hold it for too long, and you watch all options close before you, and what once looked so simple now swirls as unpatterned chaos.

"Do you think she'll give up the kid?" Carl B asked.

"Of course, she will," O'Bryan said. "Most of yours didn't even sleep on it."

Morning: the woman goes topside, and the Sisters chose Matthias to be the baby's matron. But that was not the biggest news of the day.

O'Bryan was going to Ascend.

We were told in school, O'Bryan with the rest of us. "My birthday's eight months away."

Sister Adelaide raised her clipboard but didn't look at it. "Incorrect," she said. "The smoke must be addling your mind." She offered a pursed-lip smile. "Congratulations."

"Really?" said O'Bryan, a hand on his heart. "Really?"

The baby—papoosed to Matthias's chest with yoga pants and jumper cables—stirred. Matthias put his pinky finger (the tip still black with frostbite) into the baby's toothless mouth, and we all watched as the baby sucked itself into silence. Even Sister Adelaide's softened into something almost human. Against all expectation, I felt an overwhelming sense of sorrow for Matthias, that he was so obviously fit for a life other than the one he had.

O'Bryan cleared his throat and turned his attention back to Sister Adelaide. "When?"

"Ten minutes," she said. "You may choose your closest friend to Ascend you."

O'Bryan rose slowly, coming to terms with what the next six hundred seconds would bring. He walked to the front of the classroom while Sister Adelaide began drawing the periodic table on the blackboard.

"Tick tock," she said, "you little sinners."

"Well," he said, "I want Eric. And Ronny." The two boys stood up and joined him at the front. "And, of course, Percy and Suze." He then called my name, Jason's, Simon's.

"Lenny, my winger, get up here, man." O'Bryan started to cry. "And I need my boys Carl Big, Carl Mids, and Carly Cue." We stood at the classroom's front to stare at Matthias and the baby alone in the desks.

"You'll say goodbye to me?" O'Bryan asked as his voice cracked along the edges.

Matthias nodded, his head in a tight bobble. And O'Bryan said his name.

Sister Adelaide was at the blackboard and double-counting her squares. I expected her to turn around, realize how many people O'Bryan had called, and revoke his privileges of having anyone at all. But when she had finished parcelling the 118 squares of the known universe, she looked over her shoulder, and then back at her board. "Everyone," she said, "is in such a hurry to leave."

We then became engulfed in a smell so putrid that I could no longer breathe. My eyelids squinted, and Carl C dry-heaved. It was the smell of burning flesh.

"I'm sorry," Matthias said, unknotting the papoose. "She needs a change."

O'Bryan didn't ask for the Nason Jr room, nor the Standing Bear, nor even the Velvet. He asked for it to be outside, at the top of the stairs that overlooked the rink. It was a kind gesture. The top of the stairs was a shorter walk to the incinerator, and there'd be no cleanup. The wind was blowing sleet that would grow to a storm by the afternoon, and everything red would return white.

The sun had not yet risen, but Sister Adelaide refused us permission to use our headlamps due to the shortage of AAAS. Instead, she carried the lone kerosene lantern as she led us single-file through the drifts.

At the top of the stairs, Sisters Harriette and Jillian were waiting, and we semicircled behind O'Bryan as he knelt in the snow, overlooking the rink, overlooking the world.

Eric was carrying the axe, and Sister Jillian gestured for him to approach, and he held the axe high above O'Bryan's head.

Sister Jillian began: "Do you, O'Bryan Shelley Turnville, confirm that you have lived without sin?"

I had seen this countless before.

"That you have acted in obeisance with hallowed law?"

But this time something was amiss.

"That you consider yourself worthy to Ascend to the Kingdom of Heaven?"

The words were the same, but they felt different.

"And that I, a Holy Sister of Perpetual Mercy, anointed as the arbitrator of the soul, have no reason to believe otherwise?"

"I do," O'Bryan said, and Eric fell the axe deep into his best friend's skull, and there was the mohawk of blood, a couple of convulsions, and that inexplicable choking sound, before O'Bryan crumpled into himself. Someone was softly crying, and I assumed it was the baby until I looked around and realized that Matthias hadn't returned from changing her. It would be lifetimes before I saw them again: the baby—of course—would be unrecognizable, but Matthias had hardly changed: his hair still falling over his eyes, his fingertips still black with frostbite, his chin still receding into his neck when he cried.

But at the time, standing knee-deep in the snow at the top of the stairs, I hardly noticed his absence. All I could focus on was O'Bryan—or, rather, what was once O'Bryan.

With most pilgrims, there was this ecstasy that filled the room, this blissed-out joy that lingered even after you've wiggled out the blade. You could see it in their faces, their white teeth shining through the red, a smile that wouldn't fade until it melted. But with O'Bryan, there was only a pile of rags. And I remembered what Suzy had told me about watching Kendra's Ascension. And I saw it too: nothing.

Mother Superior Pamela came plodding across the field, followed closely by Sister Martha, the two of them hiking up their gowns above the drifts.

Mother Superior Pamela cut through our semicircle to Sister Adelaide and whispered in her ear. Sister Adelaide nodded, and both nuns looked at me.

"Happy birthday," Mother Superior Pamela smiled. "We almost missed it."

"I'm fourteen?" I said.

Both nuns shook their heads. "No," Mother Superior Pamela said. "You're eighteen."

A cork was pulled from the base of my skull, and all the blood drained from my face. "O'Bryan and I aren't born on the same day."

"It's a leap year," Mother Superior Pamela said. "That's why we almost missed it."

From behind her, Sister Martha said, "Our records do not lie."

I began to cry. Mother Superior Pamela knelt before me and put both hands on my cheeks.

"I'll do it," I whispered to her. "I'll Ascend you."

With her thumbs she wiped away my tears as her own eyes welled. "I believe you," she said. "But the problem is, I also don't."

Her hands were incredibly warm, incredibly soft, and had the slight smell of lavender, something from that lotion a pilgrim brought us years ago.

"Listen to me," she said, her voice so low that only I could hear it. "You can either go now with a clean soul or Run Away and never go at all."

What happened next felt as if it were happening far removed, like I was peering out from deep within the moment, from the centre of my very core. The snow crunched beneath my snow pants as I knelt. Someone removed my toque and the wind was cold against my neck. Mother Superior Pamela asked me who I wanted to cleave my soul from my body, and when I found myself unable to answer, I heard Suzy's voice. I heard the snow squeal as she walked behind me, and I heard everyone hold their breath as the blade hovered. A puck about to drop.

I heard Mother Superior Pamela ask me the questions of Ascension.

And I heard myself say, "I do." And I saw a shadow trot through the tree line. And I heard the sound of metal slamming into skull.

The smell of smoke.

The taste of rust.

Someone was yelling, "I granted it! I granted it!"

I looked over my shoulder, afraid that if I moved too quickly my head would fall off.

Sister Adelaide was shaking Sister Martha by the shoulders. "She asked forgiveness! And I granted it! You heard it too!"

But Sister Martha's face was shocked empty of emotion, her eyes wide at Mother Superior Pamela, who was at Suzy's feet, the axe handle growing out her face. Sister Jillian lunged at Suzy but lost her footing in the snow, and there came a whistling so loud that it drowned out Sister Adelaide's screaming. We looked up to a bright line of purple that thickened and thickened until it was upon us and we were cast in its light as it smashed into the rink and a thousand shards of ice shrapnelled through the air. Another streak hit the nearby forest, throwing fire and boulders and entire tree trunks, and a branch javelined through Percy's throat.

Everyone scattered but the snow was deep. The air vibrated, and another crash. Another and another. The whole convent aflame.

Sister Adelaide, crawled atop the body of Mother Superior Pamela, kissing where the blade met the mush of her mouth.

Eric grabbed the handle, heaved out the axe, and held the glinting light above his head. Suzy burrowed into the snow, and from the forest, came an inhuman scream. All above us, the clouds were cut by bright streaks of light, each one on its way to explode against the earth, each one the colour of a human soul.

ACKNOWLEDGEMENTS

Some of these stories, in one form or another, first appeared elsewhere: "Perfection" was published in *Numero Cinq*; "Hello, Horse" and "What Descends When the Lake Thaws" were published in *The Fiddlehead*; "Patron Saints" was published in the inaugural issue of *Camel*; "Gravity" was published in *Geist*; "Our Overland Offensive to the Sea" in *subTerrain*; "The Great and the Gone" and "The Unitarian Church's Annual Young Writer's Short Story Competition" were published in *The New Quarterly*; "Ghost Town" was published in *Grain*. My sincerest thanks to the editors of these magazines.

"Hello, Horse" won the Alberta Writers' Guild's Howard O'Hagan Award for Short Story (2019); "The Unitarian Church's Annual Young Writer's Short Story Competition" won the National Magazine Award for Fiction (2017); "Ghost Town" won the Norma Epstein Foundation Award for Creative Writing (2018); "Gravity" was shortlisted for the National Magazine Award for Fiction (2017); "Satellite" was shortlisted for the *Malahat Review's* novella contest (2020).

Several writers aided in editing this manuscript. They are (in order of beauty): Donna Williams, Suzette Mayr, Don Gillmor, Clarissa Hurley, Veronique Darwin, Andrew Wood, Aritha van Herk, Micheal Prior, Mikka Jacobsen, Mark Anthony Jarman, and Jordan Kroeger. Thank you, thank you.

John Metcalf. Helluva editor. Helluva guy. It has been an honour and a privilege.

I regard the staff at Biblioasis as the coterie of unsung saints.

Funding for this project was provided by the Banff Centre for the Arts, the University of New Brunswick, the University of Calgary, the Alberta Foundation for the Arts, and the Canada Council for the Arts. My gratitude to the taxpayers of the nation.

My love and respect to Mom, Dad, Tress, and Sullivan. This collection was inspired by Maisy and is dedicated to Litia.